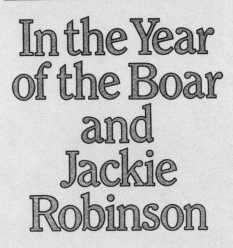

In the Year of the Boar and Jackie Robinson

Bette Bao Lord

In the Year of the Boar and Jackie Robinson

ILLUSTRATIONS BY

Marc Simont

🔥 HarperTrophy®
A Division of HarperCollins Publishers

To my mother and father

Harper Trophy® is a registered trademark
of HarperCollins Publishers Inc.

In the Year of the Boar and Jackie Robinson
Text copyright © 1984 by Bette Bao Lord
Illustrations copyright © 1984 by Marc Simont
All rights reserved. No part of this book may be
used or reproduced in any manner whatsoever
without written permission except in the case of
brief quotations embodied in critical articles and
reviews. For information address HarperCollins
Children's Books, a division of HarperCollins
Publishers, 10 East 53rd Street, New York, NY 10022.
Printed in the U.S.A.

Library of Congress Cataloging-in-Publication Data
Lord, Bette.
    In the Year of the Boar and Jackie Robinson.

    Summary: In 1947, a Chinese child comes to
Brooklyn, where she starts to feel at home and to
make friends when she discovers baseball and the
Brooklyn Dodgers.
    [1. Chinese American–Fiction.   2. Moving,
Household—Fiction.   3. Schools—Fiction]   I.
Simont, Marc, ill.   II. Title.
PZ7.L8773In   1984   [Fic]   83-48440
ISBN 0-06-024003-2
ISBN 0-06-024004-0 (lib. bdg.)

(A Harper Trophy Book)
ISBN 0-06-440175-8 (pbk.)

Contents

一

月

JANUARY

Chinese New Year

In the Year of the Dog, 4645, there lived halfway across the world from New York a girl called Sixth Cousin. Otherwise known as Bandit.

One winter morning, a letter arrived at the House of Wong from her father, who had been traveling the four seas. On the stamp sat an ugly, bald bird. The paper was blue. When Mother read it, she smiled. But the words made Grandmother cry and Grandfather angry. No one gave Sixth Cousin even the smallest hint of why.

It is so unfair, she thought. Must I drool like Chow Chow, eyeing each mouthful until someone is good and ready to toss a scrap my way? If Father was here, he'd tell. He would never treat me like a child, like a girl, like a nobody.

Still, Bandit dared not ask. How many times had she been told that no proper member of an upright Confucian family ever questioned the conduct of elders? Or that children must wait until invited to speak? Countless times. Only the aged were considered wise. Even the opinion of her father, the youngest son of the Patriarch, did not matter. No wonder he had gone away to seek his fortune.

She tried to pretend nothing had happened, but it was hard. All day, the elders behaved unnaturally in her presence. No unintended slights, quick nods, easy smiles, teasing remarks or harsh words. They were so kind, *too* kind. Bandit felt as if she had sprouted a second head, and they were all determined to ignore politely the unsightly growth.

That evening, as she and Fourth Cousin sat on the bed playing pick-up-beans, she confided in her best friend. "Something's happened. Something big has happened!"

"Oh?" said the older girl. "You are always imagining things! Remember the time you told everyone there was a goldfish swimming in the bamboo trees? It was only a fallen kite. Remember the time you overheard the cook plotting to murder the washerwoman? He was only sharpening his cleaver to kill a hen."

Bandit scowled as she scattered the dried lima beans. "That was then. Now is now!"

"All right, all right," sighed her dearest friend. "What has happened now?"

"That's it. I don't know," she answered.

"Well then, let's play. My turn. Sixies."

"No!" shouted Bandit, grabbing the other girl's hands. "Think! Think! What would make Mother smile, Grandmother cry and Grandfather angry?"

Fourth Cousin shrugged her shoulders and began to unbraid her hair. She was always fussing with her hair.

Bandit thought and thought, annoyed at her friend's silence, sorry that no matter how Fourth Cousin tried she would never be pretty.

Soon the coals in the brazier were dying, and suddenly the room was cold. The cousins scrambled under the covers. The beans tumbled onto the floor. Bandit knew she should pick them up, but she just stayed put. She had thinking to do.

Finally Bandit had the answer. Fourth Cousin was asleep.

"Wake up! Wake up!"

"Mmmmmmmmmmm?"

"Listen. I've got it. Remember the time the enemy planes bombed the city for two straight days and we had to hide in the caves with only hard-boiled eggs to eat? What happened when we came home?"

"Who cares?"

"Father brought us that pony of a dog. Mother thought it was cute and smiled. But Grandmother was frightened and cried and hid behind the moon gate. And Grandfather was very angry. He said, 'Youngest Son, are you mad? Unless you mean for us to eat that beast, take him away. Take him away this minute.' His voice was as cold as the northwest wind." Bandit stood up and threaded her hands into her sleeves as Grandfather did. She cleared her throat the way he did whenever he was displeased, and stomped up and down the bed.

Fourth Cousin never opened an eye. She turned on her side and curled up like a shrimp.

Bandit pounced on her. "Don't you see? Father is bringing the dog back."

"Never!"

Bandit thought it over and sighed. "You're right. You're always right." Quietly, very quietly, she slipped under the covers.

Sleep still would not come. Bandit heard the sounds of laughter and voices, footfalls and bicycle bells, as guests departed from one court, then another. It was the season for merrymaking, when the New Year approaches and old debts are paid. At last the lanterns along the garden walk were snuffed out, and the room was dark. Bandit reached out. Fourth Cousin's hand was warm.

Through the wall came the faint strains of a song. Mother was playing Father's record again.

The music carried Bandit away, thousands of miles to the sea. Its waters were not muddy like the River of Golden Sands that churned at the bottom of the Mountain of Ten Thousand Steps on which the House of Wong was perched. The sea was calm; deep green like jade. As far as the heavens, the skies soared. In the distance, something blue. A boat in the shape of a bird. Slowly it floated toward shore. She shaded her eyes to get a better look. On the deck was Father. She shouted and waved, but he did not seem to hear.

"Father! Father!" She shouted until she was hoarse. Then she ran into the sea, forgetting she could not swim. Soon he was just a fingertip away. "Father! Father!"

Her cries angered the sleeping demons of the deep and they sent a wall of water to quiet the intruder. . . .

Splash! She awoke. Her face was wet.

"Look what you've made me do, you Bandit!"

She sat up to find Fourth Cousin gone and Awaiting Marriage, the servant, sprawled on the floor. Beside the old woman was a shattered water urn. All about, the offending beans.

Before Bandit could apologize, Awaiting Marriage screwed up her skinny face and wailed. The sight was ugly enough to frighten the devil himself. Cook was right. One hundred wedding trunks could not buy Awaiting Marriage even a hunchbacked, lame-footed husband.

"Bandit, I've got you this time. This time you have to answer to your grandmother. I'm going to show

her the pieces!" The servant stood up, shaking a frag-
ment in Bandit's face.

Bandit brushed her hand away. "It's nothing but
crockery. No Ming urn!"

Awaiting Marriage squeezed out a wicked smile.
"Aha! You've forgotten it's New Year's time. Yes, Bandit, New Year's time." Giggling, the servant scurried
out.

Amitabha! Bandit was in trouble, deep trouble.
Grandmother was the Matriarch of the House of
Wong. What she ordered was always done. What she
said was always so. How many times had she warned
against breaking things during the holidays? It would
bring bad luck, bad luck for the next three hundred
and sixty-five days. And if anything made Grandmother unreasonable, it was bad luck.

Quickly, Bandit got out of bed, used what was left
in Fourth Cousin's water urn to wash, dressed, plaited
her hair and then began seriously to clean the room.
That was another of Grandmother's dictums. Not a
speck of dust. Not a misplaced article. Everything must
be in harmony to welcome the New Year.

As she was straightening out the shoes in the bottom
of the tall rosewood bureau, Awaiting Marriage ap-

peared at the door. She grinned as if greeting the matchmaker. "Young Mistress," she said, gloating. "Young Mistress, the Matriarch wishes to see you in her quarters."

"Now?"

"Now." With an extravagant bow, the tattletale removed herself.

Bandit felt as if she had been summoned by an irate emperor. This time the punishment would be more than harsh words or three strokes of a bamboo cane. Much more. But she had to obey. No one ever disobeyed the Matriarch. Quickly she ran to the washstand and tucked a towel inside the seat of her pants. Still . . . there must be some way to soften Grandmother's heart. She must think. And quickly, before another offense was added to the first. Think. Who could help?

Yes, of course, naturally. Ninth Cousin, otherwise known as Precious Coins. He was the baby of the clan. The favored grandchild. Whenever Bandit needed a few pennies to buy melon seeds or candied plums, she sent Precious Coins to ask Grandmother for them. The Matriarch never refused him. If he would shed a bucket of tears for Bandit, perhaps her life would be spared.

Where could that fat boy be? He hated to walk, loved being carried. With all the cousins getting ready for the festivities, he was probably still sitting on his bed like a buddha, waiting for a pair of feet.

She ran out the door, along the gallery past Mother's room, through the rock garden into the next court, which belonged to Third Uncle. She tiptoed past his study. Uncle hated to be disturbed when he was doing accounts. And that's all he ever did. She heard him muttering as he clicked the beads on his abacus, figuring out new ways to pocket a cent. Poor Third Aunt. No matter how she screamed and schemed, her husband refused to loosen his purse strings. Unlike Father, he never squandered money for gifts. But he seldom reaped joy either.

Precious Coins was sitting on his bed. As soon as Bandit stepped into his room, he held out his arms. She could not resist giving him a big hug. He was cute as a dumpling and just as round.

"See Grandmother now?"

"Yes. But no pennies today. When I set you down, you must hold on to my leg. Don't let go, no matter what. A new game, see?"

"Hold leg. No let go."

"If you let go, you lose."

"No let go." Precious Coins held up his arms again.

Scooping him up, she walked slowly along the pathway past the lotus pond and crossed the half-moon bridge to the Matriarch's quarters.

At the threshold, Bandit hesitated. What took more courage—to enter or to run away? Inside sat all the women of the older generation, even Grand-grand-grand Auntie, who was ninety-three. It only proved Grandmother's warning to be true. Bad luck. It was already here.

"Granddaughter, you may come in."

Holding Precious Coins even tighter, Bandit inched toward the carved ebony chair in the center of the room. She kept her eyes on Grandmother's bound feet, which rested on a stool.

She set the boy down. At once he plopped to the floor and put his arms around her left leg.

"Good morning, Grandmother," she whispered, still keeping her eyes on Grandmother's feet. They were very tiny, like little red peppers.

"Look at me, child. I have something important to say."

One hundred lashes? Ten thousand characters to copy? One hundred thousand hours in her room? If only she had picked up the beans.

Blinking away the tears, Bandit looked up. Her eyes met the Matriarch's. No one spoke. Bandit looked around, searching for a friendly face among the women. No one smiled. Not even Mother.

"Granddaughter, today is one of the saddest days in my long life, in all our lives. You, my sixth grandchild, must go away, far away. . . ."

No! How can I? Bandit thought. I am too young. Who will take care of me? A tear fell, then another.

"Grandmother," she begged. "Let me have another chance. I will be careful. I will never, ever, as long as I live, break another thing during the holidays. I promise. Please don't send me away."

"What are you talking about? I am not sending you away. You are going away because your father has sent for you and your mother. He has decided not to return to Chungking. He plans to make America his home. Your grandfather has agreed."

The letter! No wonder Mother had smiled, Grandmother had cried and Grandfather had been so angry. Oh, Father, she thought. At long last, we'll be together again!

Bandit could not help smiling. She was brimful of happiness. But then she saw the sadness on Grandmother's face and ran to comfort her.

Boom! Bandit fell. True to his word, Precious Coins had not let go of her leg.

Then all the women of the House of Wong gathered around to fuss over her.

"Oh, you poor thing!" they cried. "What's to become of you?"

"Exiled like a criminal to a distant land."

"With no clan to nurture you. Surrounded by strangers."

"Strangers who aren't even Chinese."

"And those cowboys and Indians. What kind of place is that for a child to grow up in? Dodging bullets and arrows?"

"You'll starve! Imagine eating nothing but warm puppies and raw meat!"

"How will you become civilized? America does not honor Confucius. America is foreign, so foreign."

On and on they went, wailing like paid mourners at a funeral. But Bandit was not afraid. She had faith in her father. Nothing awful will happen, she told herself. No bad luck. The Year of the Boar would bring travel, adventure and double happiness.

The final day of the Year of the Dog lasted until dawn. No one slept. Not even Precious Coins. For tradition had long decreed that a bad dream on any New Year's Eve was an omen of bad tomorrows. To make sure no one had a nightmare, all the beds in the House of Wong stood empty until the skies were lit by the dawn and the danger passed.

The lofty Hall of Ancestors was festooned with holiday banners and graced with clansmen from near and far. They formed clusters of color like the glass pieces in a kaleidoscope. Everyone's gown was of bright silk or brocade, and many were embroidered with gold and silver threads and lined in fur, or stitched with sequins and pearls.

A few gowns, like Bandit's, betrayed the twelve-course dinner the clansmen had consumed earlier. It did not matter. At the New Year's feast no one ever scolded, even if a barbarian should wash his face in the soup. A few faces, like Bandit's, could use a washing, even in soup. They were streaked with ash, for they had leaned too close to the sizzle of firecrackers. But even so, no cross words. On New Year's Eve, exceptions were the rule.

Gamblers seated at a dozen tables chatted and cheered as they vied at mah-jongg, cards and rhyming couplets, while would-be singing warriors and courtesans tagged after the tunes the musicians played and the servants, spinning like tops, circled the floor with drinks and delicacies. At each stop they collected a generous tip. Near daybreak of New Year's Day, even Third Uncle forgot himself.

Before the altar, which was laden with offerings for the ancestors, Grandfather sat, telling stories to the very old and the very young.

Many in his audience were fighting sleep. Their stomachs were filled with sweets . . . their pockets with red envelopes containing money from the elders . . . their heads with stories of monkey kings and fox fairies, noble ministers and celestial fools, loyal sons, forgetful magpies, the weaving maid who lived on the far side of the River of Stars. No wonder they drooped.

Not Bandit. She was wide awake, sitting cross-legged holding hands with Grand-grand Uncle and his wife of sixty years who, for as long as Bandit could recall, had refused to address her husband. Both the old artist and the former beauty had long forgotten his misdeed. The date of it, however, was enshrined in memory, and dubbed "Foul Friday." Perhaps, in the beginning, the wife might have relented. Then it became unthinkable. Now, in his old age, Grand-grand Uncle delighted in painting Grand-grand Auntie's portrait. Sometimes with warts. Sometimes with big feet or donkey grins. Always fanciful. Bandit thought each picture worth ten thousand laughs. Secretly she collected them, whispering to Grand-grand Auntie that she did so on her behalf. Thus, both artist and subject adored her. Thus, Bandit had become their official go-between.

". . . And so finally the worthy peasant could sleep peacefully in his grave."

Everyone applauded. Glancing up at the feuding husband and wife, Bandit saw tears in their eyes. If only, she thought, if only they could be friends again before I go away. Then they will not need a go-between. For the first time, Bandit felt a little bit sad to be going away.

Grandfather tapped his pipe on the arm of his chair, calling for attention. Suddenly, the Hall was still.

"It is almost time to go to bed, my clansmen. But before we can, there is something we must do. Sixth Cousin, rise and come to my side."

Bandit jumped to her feet and obeyed. Grandfather was the Patriarch of the clan, even more powerful than Grandmother. Everyone was now looking her way. Bandit blushed.

"Now, now, my child," Grandfather said with a smile, "since when have you become so shy?"

Everyone laughed, the cousins the loudest.

Tapping his pipe again, Grandfather continued. "As you know, my youngest son's wife and daughter will be leaving us this week. There will still be time enough to say a proper good-bye. But we must not send Sixth Cousin away without giving her an official name. Bandit will not do, will it?"

"No!" shouted the House of Wong.

"So, tell me my child, do you have a preference?"

"I, Grandfather?"

"Who else?"

Bandit looked to the rafters, as if a hint might be hidden there. Everyone waited quietly. Finally she replied, "Grandfather, since I am going to America, I would like an American name."

Some nodded approval. Others shook their heads. An American name!

Grandfather stroked his white beard. Then he said, "American name it is."

Now everyone nodded approval.

Bandit clapped. Fourth Cousin did too. My dearest friend, Bandit thought. I wish you were going with us. Again, she felt sad.

"Any suggestions, my child?" Grandfather asked.

She had not been prepared for that! Everyone knew she did not speak English, but if she admitted it now everyone would enjoy a big laugh just the same. She looked at the rafters again. I must know an American name, she thought. I must.

Suddenly one came to her.

"How about Uncle Sam?" she shouted.

All laughed until some cried.

Bandit felt that her face was as red as a fried lobster.

Grandfather came to her rescue. "I, myself, do not care for the sound of it. How about something more melodious?"

Think! She must know another American name. Then it came to her. Yes, that was it. Everyone loved her movies. She was just about the most famous movie star in all the world.

"Shirley Temple!"

For a minute no one moved. Then Grandfather applauded. Then so did everyone else.

Grandfather tapped his pipe once more, calling the clansmen to order. Straightening his back, he pronounced the official words. "I, as Patriarch, do hereby advise my clansmen that my sixth grandchild, the thirty-third member of the House of Wong now living under the ancestral roofs, and one of the thirty-ninth generation registered in the Clan Book, will now be known as Shirley Temple Wong."

二
月

FEBRUARY

A Journey of Ten Thousand Miles

The sea was not calm, nor deep green like jade. It writhed like a fierce, black dragon with chili peppers up its snout. And Shirley never saw the skies. She lingered in her bunk throughout the month-long journey to San Francisco, with no appetite for food, much less adventure.

Mother, though, never faltered. As giant waves sent slippers, suitcases, tables and the chair she sat in slithering to and fro across the floor, she knit on, unperturbed. If she did cry out, it was not because she had crashed into the wall but because she had dropped a stitch.

Father had always claimed that his wife was like no other. It was true. Mother was unique. Everyday things like the tiniest cockroach or a gentle tap on the back made her shriek. Extraordinary things did not alarm her. Shirley knew better than to ask Mother to remove a splinter. Even a droplet of blood made her cringe. Yet when Precious Coins was about to be born and the hospital miles away with bombs falling like hailstones, it was Mother alone who soothed the frantic household and quietly delivered the baby. And now . . . now she who had never dared go even to the nearest market without a companion had taken charge of their journey of ten thousand miles.

At last the ocean ended, and the ship hiccupped to a halt at the harbor. *Amitabha!* The queasiness was gone. Shirley felt like Shirley again, not like a sick toad.

"Hurry!" Mother said, taking her by the hand. "We must not miss the train."

Shirley could hardly keep up with her as she snaked her way through the crowd of travelers. At every stop, whether immigration or customs, she alone gave the magic password, for not once did they have to fill out extra forms, not once were their bags opened. All the inspectors seemed bewitched by the lovely, slim Chinese woman who was in such a hurry.

Outside, there was a torrential rain. Somehow Mother found a taxi and it delivered them to the station not a minute too soon.

Only when they were safe in their compartment, when nothing serious could go wrong, did Mother fret. "What if your father is not there to meet us?"

"But you wrote."

"What if the letter was lost?"

"You sent three."

"I did?"

"You told me so yourself."

"What if I made a mistake in the address?"

"You couldn't have. Not on all three."

The what-ifs continued, and Shirley tried not to smile. It was so like Mother to tame a den of tigers and then jump at the sound of a kitten's meow.

Throughout the journey across the United States, Shirley stared out the window of the train. But she remembered nothing of what she saw. Her thoughts were always with Father. Father, who knew how everything worked. Was he not an engineer with a diploma from Shanghai to prove it? Had he not explained why the stars twinkled and how submarines slunk beneath the seas? When she asked why people must die, he had said, "Because we must make room and give others a turn to live." And he could fix anything. Lamps that refused to light. Doors that squeaked. Even quarrels, except for the one between Grand-grand Aunt and Grand-grand Uncle.

How she missed him!

As the wheels of the train clacked along the tracks, they seemed to chant—*Four more days, just four more days. . . . Three days, just three days. . . . Only two, only two, only two. . . . Tomorrow, tomorrow. . . . Today!*

At last it was the hour when their year-long separation would end. Shirley clutched her seat, afraid joy would launch her through the ceiling and whisk her high above the clouds. She fixed her gaze on Mother, who twisted her handkerchief nervously, smiling at someone who was not yet there.

"Can we go now?"

"Better wait till the train has come to a stop. You wouldn't want to fall and skin a knee just before you see Father."

"I'll be careful."

"We will be there soon enough."

"Now?"

"The train is slowing down. Soon."

"Now?"

"Now."

Hand in hand they made their way down the crowded aisle toward the exit, peering out the windows at the people waiting on the platform.

"There he is!" Mother whispered.

"Where?"

"By the far pillar."

"I see him. Father! Father!"

Shirley freed herself and burrowed through the passengers to the door. Leaping off the train, she ran to the dapper man in a bow tie.

He lifted her into his arms and swung her about, hugging her tightly. "What disgraceful behavior!" he exclaimed in a mocking tone so familiar that it made her teary. "Has your mother taught you no shame— embracing in public? Who are you anyway?"

"Father, it's me. Shirley. Shirley Temple Wong."

He shook with laughter. "Shirley? Where did you get such a name?"

She started to explain, but suddenly he was still. He set her down. Before them stood Mother. Her face looked so solemn. His did too. Something was happening. Mother did not blink when a man smashed a bottle nearby. Father did not react when another jostled him. For a long moment, Mother and Father simply glowed, as if they were caught in a spell.

Father bowed. "It is good that you are here, my wife."

"It is good to be here, my husband." Mother, too, bowed.

Taking one of Father's hands in her left and one of Mother's in her right, Shirley jumped up and down. "Take us home, Father. Take us home."

Home was Brooklyn, New York, but Shirley would not know that for a while. To her, it was simply *Mei Guo*, Beautiful Country.

In the taxi her parents talked in whispers while Shirley ogled the tall buildings. But no matter how she scrunched, she could not see if their roofs curved skyward like the temples of China or were topped with straw like the homes of peasants. Now and then she

waved, even though the streets, as wide and as straight as the airstrip in Chungking, were empty. Where were the bicycles and rickshaws, the mules and the carts? How did people market? There were no peddlers or farmers' stalls. But strangest of all, where were all the people? In Chungking, there were always people. Surely somebody lived in those tall buildings. Surely. Shirley could not know that it was Sunday, a day when everyone stayed put, except to go to Church, and the tall buildings held only offices.

As the taxi approached the Brooklyn Bridge, Shirley gasped. She wanted to jump out and touch it. Never had she seen anything like it before, not even in pictures. How was it held upright? Surely not by the ropes that looked like Mother's knitting stretched out.

Sometimes Shirley wondered why she was not afraid. But there was too much magic in this new place for her to question it. And besides, she was with Father. Once more she took his hand.

Soon after crossing the bridge, the taxi stopped. The houses here were short, just a few stories high. They were built of stone and they all looked exactly alike. They stood directly on the street, unprotected by garden walls. Steps leading to doors went up and down from the ground.

"We are here!" Father announced.

Shirley's new home was on the third floor. Altogether, the place was barely larger than her own room had been in the clan compound. But her disappointment did not last, for Father was so proud of it.

"Look at these walls," he boasted. "I spent an entire week cleaning every inch with a scouring pad."

A sofa and a chair covered in a faded floral pattern sagged where people had sat. Set against the wall was a square table and three straight-backed chairs, chairs without dragon feet. In the middle of the room was a plain, unlacquered screen. It hid the only purchase Father had made, a brass bed for two.

"Where will I sleep, Father?"

"Ah!" Father opened a door. "For you, my daughter, a most special place." Behind the door was a place with drawers up to the ceiling on both sides. Pulling out the bottom ones, he flipped them over and set them side by side, then placed three cushions over them. "A fine bed for you. Try it."

Shirley lay down.

"I knew it." Father beamed. "Just your size."

Shirley nodded, although she wondered what would happen if she grew another inch. Perhaps Father thought she had attained her full height.

"Come along, I'll show you the kitchen."

It did not look at all like a kitchen. No hanging ducks or hams. No woodpile or soot. No picture of the Kitchen God. Just a tiny room with a washing bowl and two white boxes.

"Where is the cook?" Mother asked.

This time Father's crooked smile was even more crooked than usual. "In America, all cooks work in restaurants."

Must we eat out for every meal? Shirley wondered.

"In America," Father continued, "the wife cooks."

Then we shall starve, Shirley thought. Unlike the Aunties, Mother had never had any interest in preparing food.

Father opened the bigger of the white boxes. "It's easy. Everything needed is in here." Eggs hung in the door, bottles with colored fluids stood on a shelf. There were beans, spinach and oranges in one drawer, slabs of meat in another.

Peeking inside, Shirley got goose bumps from the cold. But she couldn't find the window. She tugged Father's coat. "I don't see the window to the outside," she said.

Father laughed. "This, Shirley Temple Wong, is an ice box. A machine that cools food and keeps it from spoiling. In America you only have to market once a week, not every day."

"And I suppose," Mother said, "in America the wife does that, too."

"That's right."

For a moment, Shirley thought Mother was going to cry. But she didn't. Instead, after a while, she said, "Well then, I shall learn to cook and shop."

"And launder, too, my wife. But for cooking and washing you will have help."

Mother sighed. "Thank Buddha for the servant."

"No, no. Not that kind of help." Smiling as he did whenever he was about to reveal a wonderful secret, Father struck a match and put it to the top of the second white box. *Poof!* Out came blue fire. Off went Mother to hug the wall.

"A stove fit for a banquet!" Father laughed. Shirley dared not.

Father opened another door. Behind it was what Shirley recognized as a tiny room for bathing, even though the tub was neither tall nor round nor of wood. It was white, and inside it stood a large, metallic can. Father took out a hose and attached it to the nozzle at one end of the tub and then, twisting a knob, called forth water that filled the metal can to overflowing.

"Watch carefully," he said, looking up with that smile again.

Mother stepped backward, but Shirley, anxious to prove her mettle, leaned forward an inch.

"Are you watching?"

The new arrivals nodded uncertainly as he dumped a cupful of blue powder into the water. Then, with a flourish, he plugged the attached wire into the wall.

Chug! Chug! Chug! The metal can bounced, banging against the walls of the tub like a squat madman foaming at the mouth.

The sight sent Mother out of the room.

"What is it?" Shirley finally asked, hoping not to appear ignorant, but hoping more that the thing would not escape the confines of the tub and test her resolve.

"A machine that washes."

"Washes?"

He nodded proudly.

For a moment Shirley hesitated, then decided she had better speak up. "Father, if you don't mind, I prefer to bathe alone."

To her dismay, Father doubled over with laughter. Or was it pain? It was hard to tell from the way he kept trying to tame the expression on his face each time he opened his mouth. Obviously he wanted to say something, but could only make noises that sounded like sobs. Again and again he shook his head at his foolish child. Too foolish, obviously, to appreciate such a marvel. One that must have cost him hundreds of dollars. Or worse yet, one that Father had invented himself.

At last, he spoke. "Not you, Bandit. Clothes."

"Clothes?"

"All types of clothes. Your mother will love it."

Shirley did not think so.

The tour finished, Father took them for a walk around the neighborhood. All the streets looked alike. Each street was flat and painted black. There were no steep hills. Each house was a replica of theirs. Every place stuck to the next. Wall to wall, without any gardens. No moon gates or fan windows or stone lions. Now and then a tree, but no flower beds. With no servants, how could there be gardens? But then, with no servants there would be no Awaiting Marriage to spoil Shirley's fun either.

Even the one bicycle she saw was strange. It had three wheels.

Only a short distance from her house were stores.

"This is for groceries," Father said. "That is for snacks. And this is the place where I buy my newspapers and cigarettes."

Shirley's stomach began to growl and they returned home. Father prepared lunch. Orange noodles out of a can. Mother smiled. "So simple. Cooking in America will be no chore at all."

When the dishes were done, friends arrived. Father introduced them as Mr. Hu, Mr. Tan, Mr. Lin and Mr. Koo. They were all men working in America, anxious for news of home and family. Eagerly they queried Mother, drinking tea and smoking cigarettes. How proudly Father looked on!

Before long, there were no more cigarettes. Father put on his coat to go out and buy more for his guests.

Then, a wonderful idea popped into Shirley's head. She would go for the cigarettes.

"Father, you stay. I'll go for the cigarettes," she said.

"You?"

"I can find my way. You pointed the store out to me this morning."

He looked pleased but skeptical.

She had to convince him. Everybody was listening. On each face, a grin, the knowing kind elders give to children. Shirley did not like it.

Father must have sensed her discomfort, for he reached for her coat and said, "Let us go together then."

"Father, please let me go by myself."

He looked toward Mother, who gave a quick but emphatic shake of the head. But before she could actually say no and ruin Shirley's plan, Shirley spoke up, twisting and turning, marking the steps as if showing off a fancy dance. "All I do is turn right at the bottom of the stairs, walk until the end of the block, then turn left until I reach the store. And to come back, I turn right, then right again to our house, which is the second from the end and has a boat painted on the hallway light."

The guests applauded.

Knowing too well that Mother would not approve of her performance, Shirley never took her eyes off Father.

He hung up his coat.

Shirley stood tall as a warrior. Once Father made up his mind, Mother would not try to change it. Even Grandfather had despaired of trying, and that's why they were in America.

Opening the door, Father said, "Say Lucky Strike."

"Rukee Sike."

"Tell the man in the store, Lucky Strike."

"Rukee Sike."

"You won't forget."

"Not I!"

With a dollar to buy four packs, Shirley started off, skipping and chanting all the way:

> "Right, left
> Rukee Sike.
> Right, right
> home."

At the store a skinny man with a big red nose welcomed her with a smile. Encouraged, she opened her mouth wide to pronounce her first English words for an American. "Rukee Sike!"

But instead of giving her the cigarettes, he rattled off a string of nonsensical sounds.

What if she couldn't make him understand?

She puffed on an imaginary cigarette and shouted again, "Rukee Sike! Rukee Sike!"

This time he nodded. Then shook his head.

What does he mean, she wondered. Yes, he understood. No, he didn't.

She was about to try again when he ran around the counter and took her by the hand to the door.

Pointing to another store across the street, he shouted even louder than she had. "Rukee Sike! Rukee Sike!"

Ah! Now she understood. Yes, her English was most proper. No, he did not have Father's brand. But . . . that other place did.

Shirley thanked the man with a low bow, then hurried across the road, blushing. How awful it would have been to have returned home without proof of her triumph!

The woman in the second store was reading a book. Without glancing up when spoken to, she plunked down one, then another, until all four packs were safely in Shirley's hands.

Simple. It was quite simple. Nothing to it at all, Shirley thought as she fingered the cellophane and walked proudly out the door. Turning right, she could almost see Father smiling at his amazing daughter as he passed cigarettes to the men, who shouted and clapped. Turning right again, she imagined Mother, teary with pride, reaching for a handkerchief. Congratulations, Shirley Temple Wong! Congratulations!

At the steps of the house second from the corner, she stopped to straighten her coat and smooth her hair. In her moment of triumph, she must look her best. Holding the cigarettes with both hands like an offering to the gods, she marched up to the front door. Something made her look through the glass beside the wooden frame. There was the hall light. But where was the painted boat?

She hurried to the street to see if indeed it was the second house from the corner. It was. Perhaps in her glory, she had not walked far enough. She ran to the next street, to another second house. Again, a hall light. But it was painted with a rose.

She rushed across the street to the house facing. No light at all. Just a lamp on a table.

Quickly Shirley retraced her steps. Her heart raced even faster than the patter of her shoes on the sidewalk. Now right. Now left. But the store had disappeared. There was just another house, like all the others.

For a while, she ran here and there, up every set of steps looking for the boat. It was getting dark.

Finally she was too tired to look anymore. She sat down on the curb. Perhaps someone would come to her rescue. But no one passed. She was alone. Her hands were stiff from the cold. Tears fell on the cellophane. She didn't care.

What had gone wrong? she asked herself. The directions were clear. Right, left, store. Right, right, home. Suddenly, she knew. She had gone to a second store and forgotten to start back from the first. Knowing did not help. She would never find the skinny man with the big red nose or the woman who read. She would never have another chance. What a fool she was! Nothing but a fool. Utterly ashamed, she hid her face in her arms.

Someone tapped her on the shoulder. Looking up, she saw Father. He offered his hand, but not a word of rebuke. Silently they walked, hand in hand. With each step she felt better. At the first corner, they met Mr. Tan. At the second, Mr. Hu. And so it went until all the guests had joined them. Not a one was unkind enough to mention why he was out roaming the streets.

As they passed the cigarette store, Father began to sing. It was a marching song, one soldiers sang when they returned victorious from battle. Everyone joined in.

Later Shirley wrote a letter to Fourth Cousin and boasted of how she had triumphed on her very first day in Brooklyn. Naturally, she did not mention the little mishap. Why worry the clan unnecessarily? She would never be lost again.

MARCH

China's Little Ambassador

Nine o'clock sharp the very next morning, Shirley sat in the principal's office at P. S. 8. Her mother and the schoolmistress were talking. Shirley didn't understand a word. It was embarrassing. Why hadn't she, too, studied the English course on the records that

Father had sent? But it was too late now. She stopped trying to understand. Suddenly, Mother hissed, in Chinese. "Stop that or else!"

Shirley snapped her head down. She had been staring at the stranger. But she could not keep her eyes from rolling up again. There was something more foreign about the principal than about any other foreigner she had seen so far. What was it? It was not the blue eyes. Many others had them too. It was not the high nose. All foreign noses were higher than Chinese ones. It was not the blue hair. Hair came in all colors in America.

Yes, of course, naturally. The woman had no eyelashes. Other foreigners grew hair all over them, more than six Chinese together. This woman had none. Her skin was as bare as the Happy Buddha's belly, except for the neat rows of stiff curls that hugged her head.

She had no eyebrows, even. They were penciled on, and looked just like the character for man, 人. And every time she tilted her head, her hair moved all in one piece like a hat.

"Shirley."

Mother was trying to get her attention. "Tell the principal how old you are."

Shirley put up ten fingers.

While the principal filled out a form, mother argued excitedly. But why? Shirley had given the correct answer. She counted just to make sure. On the day she was born, she was one year old. And two months later, upon the new year, she was two. That was the Year of the Rabbit. Then came the Dragon, Snake, Horse, Sheep, Monkey, Rooster, Dog and now it was the year of the Boar, making ten. Proof she was ten.

Mother shook her head. Apparently, she had lost the argument. She announced in Chinese, "Shirley, you will enter fifth grade."

"Fifth? But, Mother, I don't speak English. And besides, I only completed three grades in Chungking."

"I know. But the principal has explained that in America everyone is assigned according to age. Ten years old means fifth grade. And we must observe the American rules, mustn't we?"

Shirley nodded obediently. But she could not help thinking that only Shirley had to go to school, and only Shirley would be in trouble if she failed.

Mother stood up to leave. She took Shirley by the hand. "Remember, my daughter, you may be the only Chinese these Americans will ever meet. Do your best. Be extra good. Upon your shoulders rests the reputation of all Chinese."

All five hundred million? Shirley wondered.

"You are China's little ambassador."

"Yes, Mother." Shirley squared her shoulders and tried to feel worthy of this great honor. At the same time she wished she could leave with Mother.

Alone, the schoolmistress and Shirley looked at each other. Suddenly the principal shut one eye, the right one, then opened it again.

Was this another foreign custom, like shaking hands? It must be proper if a principal does it, Shirley thought. She ought to return the gesture, but she didn't know how. So she shut and opened both eyes. Twice.

This brought a warm laugh.

The principal then led her to class. The room was large, with windows up to the ceiling. Row after row of students, each one unlike the next. Some faces were white, like clean plates; others black like ebony. Some were in-between shades. A few were spotted all over. One boy was as big around as a water jar. Several others were as thin as chopsticks. No one wore a uniform of blue, like hers. There were sweaters with animals on them, shirts with stripes and shirts with squares, dresses in colors as varied as Grand-grand Uncle's paints. Three girls even wore earrings.

While Shirley looked about, the principal had been

making a speech. Suddenly it ended with "Shirley Temple Wong." The class stood up and waved.

Amitabha! They were all so tall. Even Water Jar was a head taller than she. For a fleeting moment she wondered if Mother would consider buying an ambassador a pair of high-heeled shoes.

"Hi, Shirley!" The class shouted.

Shirley bowed deeply. Then, taking a guess, she replied, "Hi!"

The teacher introduced herself and showed the new pupil to a front-row seat. Shirley liked her right away, although she had a most difficult name, Mrs. Rappaport. She was a tiny woman with dainty bones and fiery red hair brushed skyward. Shirley thought that in her previous life she must have been a bird, a cardinal perhaps. Yet she commanded respect, for no student talked out of turn. Or was it the long mean pole that hung on the wall behind the desk that commanded respect? It dwarfed the bamboo cane the teacher in Chungking had used to punish Four Hands whenever he stole a trifle from another.

Throughout the lessons, Shirley leaned forward, barely touching her seat, to catch the meaning, but the words sounded like gurgling water. Now and then, when Mrs. Rappaport looked her way, she opened and shut her eyes as the principal had done, to show friend-ship.

At lunchtime, Shirley went with the class to the school cafeteria, but before she could pick up a tray, several boys and girls waved for her to follow them. They were smiling, so she went along. They snuck back to the classroom to pick up coats, then hurried out the door and across the school yard to a nearby store. Shirley was certain they should not be there, but what choice did she have? These were now her friends.

One by one they gave their lunch money to the store owner, whom they called "Mr. P." In return, he gave each a bottle of orange-colored water, bread twice the size of an ear of corn oozing with meat balls, peppers, onions, and hot red gravy, and a large piece of brown paper to lay on the icy sidewalk and sit upon. While they ate, everyone except Shirley played marbles or cards and traded bottle caps and pictures of men swinging a stick or wearing one huge glove. It was the best lunch Shirley had ever had.

And there was more. After lunch, each of them was allowed to select one item from those displayed under the glass counter. There were paper strips dotted with red and yellow sugar tacks, chocolate soldiers in blue tin foil, boxes of raisins and nuts, envelopes of chips, cookies as big as pancakes, candy elephants, lollipops in every color, a wax collection of red lips, white teeth, pink ears and curly black mustaches. Shirley was the last to make up her mind. She chose a hand, filled with juice. It looked better than it tasted, but she did not mind. Tomorrow she could choose again.

But when she was back in her seat, waiting for Mrs. Rappaport to enter the classroom, Shirley's knees shook. What if the teacher found out about her escapade? There would go her ambassadorship. She would be shamed. Her parents would lose face. All five hundred million Chinese would suffer. Round and round in her stomach the meat balls tumbled like pebbles.

Then Mrs. Rappaport came in. She did not look pleased. Shirley flinched when the teacher went straight to the long mean pole. For the first time her heart went out to Four Hands. She shut her eyes and prayed to the Goddess of Mercy. Oh Kwan Yin, please don't let me cry! She waited, listening for Mrs. Rappaport's footsteps to become louder and louder. They did not. Finally curiosity overcame fear and she looked up. Mrs. Rappaport was using the pole to open a window!

The lessons continued. During arithmetic, Shirley raised her hand. She went to the blackboard and wrote the correct answer. Mrs. Rappaport rewarded her with a big smile. Shirley opened and shut her eyes to show her pleasure. Soon, she was dreaming about candy elephants and cookies the size of pancakes.

Then school was over. As Shirley was putting on her coat, Mrs. Rappaport handed her a letter, obviously to be given to her parents. Fear returned. Round and round, this time like rocks.

She barely greeted her mother at the door.

"What happened?"

"Nothing."

"You look sick."

"I'm all right."

"Perhaps it was something you ate at lunch?"

"No," she said much too quickly. "Nothing at all to do with lunch."

"What then?"

"The job of ambassador is harder than I thought."

At bedtime, Shirley could no longer put off giving up the letter. Trembling, she handed it to Father. She imagined herself on a boat back to China.

He read it aloud to Mother. Then they both turned

to her, a most quizzical look on their faces.

"Your teacher suggests we take you to a doctor. She thinks there is something wrong with your eyes."

四

月

APRIL

A Hungry Ghost

Day by day, week by week, little by little Shirley shrank until she was no more. It was the only explanation. Why else did the class, which had welcomed her so warmly at first, ignore her so now? True, she could only speak a few words at a time, and most often

no one could even guess at the meaning of those. True, she was a coward. Those who broke the rules to go to Mr. P's no longer bothered with her. True, she was stupid. Too stupid to know the difference between a wink and a tic until Father explained.

But still—didn't they know how lonely she felt?

It was spring now, but Shirley, hunched in her coat, walked as if there were still snow on the ground. Carefully she sidestepped the boys who played basketball, the girls who roller-skated, the groups who seemed to laugh or whisper whenever she passed. She dreaded the distance across the school yard. It was endless and full of traps. If a loose ball rolled by, should she catch it? If a girl fell, should she help her up? If someone glanced her way, should she wave? This afternoon, as every afternoon, she pretended to have somewhere to go, and hurried on. But she had nowhere to go but home.

At Mr. P's she slowed down. The pennies in her pocket jingled to be spent. But the usual crowd was pressed nose to nose at the counter, and she hurried on.

With no one to talk to, she mumbled to herself. "Buffalo . . . stink, stank, stuck . . . liberty . . .

slave . . . Mississippi Liver." She tried to string these new words with the old ones in sentences, but she had no more success than a blind man threading beads.

Ahead was a gang playing stoop ball, blocking her way. She waited for a quiet moment, when she could pass. This game was different from the others. This one she knew how to play. It was just like "Trap the Birdie," except instead of throwing up feathers stuck inside the hole of a coin, the player bounced a ball against the step and called out a mystery number. The one assigned that number had to catch the ball to win a point for his team.

Suddenly a ball flew overhead and the crowd was running toward her. She ducked inside the delicatessen next door for safety. It smelled strangely, as if packed with dirty damp socks, which upon closer inspection she recognized as cheese and fish. Not the silvery catches that swam and somersaulted in the wooden basins that lined the market at the foot of the Mountain of Ten Thousand Steps. Dead fish. So long dead that Cook would probably not even throw them out to the cats. Slivers of gray fish pickled in white glue, smoked fish with yellow eyes that bulged, raw red fish without heads or tails.

The owner spoke up.

Pointing to a pack of Juicy Fruit gum, Shirley handed him the pennies.

She waited by the door for the ball to fly in the opposite direction. When the coast was clear, she started to run across the sidewalk. Just then a voice asked, "Want to play?"

It belonged to Joseph, who sat behind her in class. His hair was always slicked down and scientifically parted in the middle. His belly protruded just enough for his hands to rest comfortably upon it. His face was pure white, as if his mother had powdered her baby on the wrong end. But to Shirley, at this moment, he was the handsomest boy in all of Brooklyn.

"Please," she said. "Please."

The other players groaned, but did nothing to stop Joseph from whispering in her ear. "You are number eight on my team."

She nodded eagerly, then bowed to all the players. They groaned again.

The next number called was hers. She ran after the ball, bumping teammates along the way, only to let it slip through her fingers. It didn't matter. She was on a team!

Her happiness did not last. No sooner had she

learned to smack the ball smartly on the steps, angling it right or left, than the other players revolted. Nobody wanted the Chinese on his team. For whenever she yelled out a mystery number, it was no mystery at all. It was always "one," or "true," or "tree." No surprise. Always "one," or "true," or "tree." In the excitement of hurling the ball, she couldn't remember how to say the higher numbers, especially after she had missed every ball when the other team called "eight." Pretty soon they were calling "eight" almost every time. Her team was losing. It was all her fault.

Finally, Joseph approached her with an outstretched hand. She shrugged, gave up the ball, and stood apart again, to watch.

She laughed along when someone missed. She cheered along when someone scored. Always a second too late, a second too long. Yet none of the gang noticed. They seemed not to see her at all. She ought to go home, she thought. Mother had learned to make delicious cupcakes. But she did not move. She stood by instead, like a hungry ghost. Finally one player left. Shirley followed a few steps behind her, pretending to kick a castaway can whenever the American turned to glance her way.

At home, she locked herself in the bathroom. Tiptoe

on the toilet seat, she peered into the mirror, trying to blow bubbles with her Juicy Fruit gum. Even the first graders blew bubbles as big as a full moon. Hers were no bigger than a button. Jaws aching, she tried again and again. She had to do something right. Had to.

"Our daughter's not herself," she heard Mother say to Father when she thought Shirley was asleep.

"She'll be fine again soon," Father said. "Even the finest engine has a few knocks at first."

But I'm not an engine, she thought. Engines don't cry. Engines don't need friends to talk to, to play with, to share. Reaching out, she tried to pretend Fourth Cousin was there.

The next day everyone was assigned a poem to recite. Shirley was not. She decided to learn one anyway. Over and over she played the new record Father had bought for her, imitating each sound until she was certain she could repeat a stanza. Then, locking herself in the bathroom, she practiced before the mirror. She gestured to the right. She gestured to the left. Not exactly certain of the meaning of the words, she dared not elaborate more. Her father, who spoke English well and tutored her, could have explained them all, but

Shirley wanted her efforts to be a complete surprise. Wait until they hear, she told herself. Just wait.

In class, she was disappointed when Mrs. Rappaport did not call for volunteers, but asked each student to recite in turn by seats. Down the first row. Up the second. At last it was Joseph's turn, and she was next. Sidling to the edge of her seat, she waited, so sure of her success that she was not even nervous. Joseph's poem seemed very long. Would it never end so she could shine?

Before he had even sat down, she popped up. Everyone murmured, wondering at the Chinese ambassador.

Shirley waited for complete silence. Then, clearing her throat, she began.

At once, they were giggling. Even Mrs. Rappaport. There was nothing to do but gesture to the right and gesture to the left, exactly as she had practiced, only faster and faster, until finally the stanza was done.

Now everyone was laughing openly. Shirley pretended to share their merriment, but tears welled in her throat and she could only manage a weak smile. What had gone wrong? Had she done something stupid again? She wanted to run, but her feet would not obey. The laughter continued. Soon she stood like a forlorn scarecrow under the pelting rain.

Mrs. Rappaport was the first to notice that Shirley was no longer smiling, and immediately clapped for order. When at last the room was still, she spoke. "Thank you for a most remarkable performance. It must have taken hours and hours to mimic each syllable just right. At first, I thought my ears were deceiving me. How is it possible? Right here in our classroom— the fabulous Donald Duck, Chip and Dale, and Mickey Mouse!"

Despite these efforts to soothe her feelings, Shirley felt humiliated. From then on, she hardly spoke, not even in Chinese to her mother. For whenever she complained, Mother would say, "Always be worthy, my daughter, of your good fortune. Born to an illustrious clan from the ancient civilization of China, you now live in the land of plenty and opportunity. By your conduct show that you deserve to enjoy the best of both worlds."

This hoary tidbit found its way to the dinner table almost as frequently as the odious glass of milk.

One night, Mother announced a plan to cheer Shirley up. When she was Shirley's age, she had pleaded with her father for permission to take piano lessons. "What?" boomed the old-fashioned scholar, who barely approved of teaching females to read and write. "What? My daughter, a singsong girl? Never!" Now she assumed that her own daughter would be overjoyed to do something she herself had never been permitted to do. She had arranged for Shirley to have piano lessons. Tomorrow after school she would go downstairs to the basement, where Señora Rodriguez, the landlady, doubled as a music teacher.

The next day, after a gentle knock, Shirley waited nervously. She had never met the Señora before, but had often seen a sinister shadow rocking back and forth behind billowing lace curtains, back and forth into the night. The door opened. There stood the Señora, short and stout, wrapped in layer upon layer of black woolen shawls. Her skin was like crinkled tissue paper; her eyes sunken and dark as well water. She smiled ever so fleetingly, as if pained by the exercise.

"Hello, how you do? I'm Shirley, and—and my mother . . ." She eked out the words as if squeezing dregs from a squashed tube of stale toothpaste. The response was less than reassuring—just a twitch of a stubby finger to follow.

She obeyed, her gaze fixed on the golden wedgies that slapped the bottom of the woman's bulging feet as she led the way through a curtain of colored beads to the piano. It, too, was covered with shawls. With a pat on the wooden bench, she invited Shirley to sit beside her. It was not going to be easy. The Señora occupied all but the tiniest sliver of the seat. Only by locking her foot around a leg of the bench did Shirley manage to stay perched.

Carefully, she twisted to face her teacher. Without a word, the Señora grimaced and out came a set of upper and lower teeth, which she then casually set on the music stand. Stuck between the molars, something green. String beans or broccoli? Shirley tried not to look, but the teeth were exactly at eye level.

Grinning like a newborn, the Señora now took Shirley's hands in hers. They felt surprisingly soft and warm, like a pair of mittens. When she finally spoke, her low, accented voice resembled the moaning of Grandmother's favorite fortune-teller, frightening and fascinating all at once.

"I weel teach these hands to make mewsic. Mewsic, the language of angels. Angels who geeve happiness to all living tings. Tings like leetle girls. Si?"

"I see."

"*Bueno.* We begin." Placing Shirley's thumb on a key, the Señora pressed it down to summon a note.

"Do. This is do." Pushing her index finger, she said, "Re. This is re." And so it went, until Shirley learned to name the white keys.

At least a hundred years seemed to have passed before Shirley could bend and unbend her stubborn fingers well enough to hit each of the eight notes of the scale without disturbing its neighbor. By then, her head ached. Her fingers ached. Her foot ached. This was not the language of angels, but the curse of demons. Did Mother not realize what she had been spared?

Just when Shirley thought the ordeal was ended, Señora Rodriguez left the room and returned with a green bird in a cage. "A leetle surprise."

The Señora set the bird on top of the piano. At once it began to squawk. "Re! Re! Re! Re!"

"Play the right note for Toscanini," the Señora suggested hurriedly.

Looking about, Shirley wondered who was to play. And who was Toscanini?

"Re! Re! Re!" The bird was flapping its wings now. "Re! Re! Re!"

Pointing to the correct key, the Señora said, "Play, leetle girl, before the birdie makes us loco."

Shirley did.

There was a glorious silence . . . but not for long.

"Fa! Fa! Fa! Fa!"

Frantically Shirley searched for fa, then played it. Relief. Then, "Mi! Mi! Mi!" And so it went, until at last a single squawk produced the desired response.

Toscanini was not impressed. On and on he

squawked while she poked at the keys. On and on until her fingers acquired a will of their own. On and on until the notes blended into a melody, a melody so compelling that Shirley and the Señora began to sway from side to side and sing along.

So enchanted were they by their duet that the miracle, at first, went unnoticed. *Amitabha!* Toscanini was speechless. Content now to perch silently on his swing, the bird kept an eye on the proceedings with an occasional three-hundred-sixty-degree flip of the head.

With the last note still in the air, Señora Rodriguez popped her teeth back inside her mouth. The lesson was over.

But the next week, Shirley's fingers seemed as clumsy as ever and now there were lessons on the piano in addition to the lessons at school. Hour after hour, day after day, week after week, study, more study, and yet again study. None of this would have truly mattered if she had had someone to walk down the long corridors at P. S. 8 with, someone to complain to about being the only Chinese in the school and the only one who had to take piano lessons, someone who cared if there was a Shirley Temple Wong in this world.

But that someone did not exist.

On the last day of school before spring vacation, she spotted a new student entering another classroom, an older Chinese girl with pigtails just like herself. Shirley hurried to greet her, but just when she was within shouting distance, the bell rang and the door closed.

All that morning, she sat at her desk unable to concentrate on what Mrs. Rappaport was teaching. She eyed the clock. Soon it would be lunchtime, she thought. Soon they would meet in the cafeteria. For once, she could speak fluently, not like an idiot. This time others, *not Shirley*, would feel left out.

She smiled, imagining the fun of talking about things the others, *not Shirley*, knew little about—things like the New Year's Parade with the dragon that flew on tall poles, the lion that pounced to the beat of the drums, the acrobats that whirled through the air, the monkeys dressed in gay costumes, and yes, of course, naturally, the blind storyteller.

When the lunch bell sounded, Shirley raced to be the first in line and waited impatiently for the new girl. Today, she did not mind when no one spoke to her.

At last, the girl came into view. Shirley rushed to

her side. *"Ni hao? Wo Jiao Shirley. Wo yeh shr Chung Kuo lai de. . . ."*

The girl looked puzzled, then shook her head, giggling. "I don't speak Chinese. I come from Chattanooga."

Laughter sped up and down the line. Shirley slunk back to her classroom. She wasn't hungry anymore.

The clansmen were right after all. America was foreign, so foreign.

During the spring recess, Shirley had nothing to do, not even homework.

"Why don't you go out and play?" suggested her mother.

"I don't feel like it."

"Would you like a cupcake?"

"I don't feel like it."

"Well, what do you feel like?"

Shirley shrugged.

At night, when she was supposedly asleep, Shirley again heard Mother whispering about her. This time Father said nothing about engines. He merely listened. Occasionally, he sighed.

On Tuesday just as Shirley and her mother were

about to wash the lunch dishes, Father suddenly burst into the apartment. In his hand, a package. On his face, that smile.

"What are you doing home so early, my husband?"

"I can't stay, but I have something here for Shirley."

"For me?"

He nodded, handing her the box.

Shirley tore it open. Inside was a pair of shiny roller skates! Before she could even give him a hug, he said, "Now, go out and play."

Out in the sunlight the air was balmy, and through skies of palest sapphire sailed clouds of gossamer silk.

As she sat on the stoop putting on her skates, Shirley dreamed of the day when she would be able to race, sashay backward and spin on one foot. Then and only then would she strap the skates together, sling them over her shoulder, and march off to join the skaters at school. They would not ignore her then, not when she could do something they could do, not when she could skate just like an American.

Skates on, she stood up. Off to the right slid one foot. Off to the left slid the other. She crashed to the sidewalk. What matter a bruise or two? Without hesitation, but only after numerous false starts, she finally succeeded in scrambling back to an upright position.

There!

Arms atwirl, she teetered forward. She tottered back. The wicked skates refused to obey and dumped her on the ground once more.

By suppertime, Shirley looked like the beggars who waited by the servants' gate for scraps from the clan table. Her clothes were torn and dirty. Her knees and elbows were bleeding. And she was no closer to becoming a skater than when she had started. Never mind. She couldn't wait for tomorrow.

Mother, however, did not share her enthusiasm. "I had no idea skating was so dangerous. You could have broken a leg, fallen unconscious, been run over by a car. Give the skates to me. Now!"

This was the droplet that broke the dam. Tears fell as Shirley handed over the skates.

"Are they so important to you?" Mother asked.

Shirley nodded.

Mother pretended to busy herself with the skates. "Well," she said gently, "perhaps when your bruises are healed and your father's not busy, he can go skating with you."

But that would not be the same.

五
月

Two Black Eyes and Wispy Whiskers

One sunny afternoon, Shirley leaned out the third-story window of P. S. 8 slapping the chalk from the class erasers. It made her cough, but she didn't mind. Doing chores was one way of thanking Mrs. Rappaport for giving her extra help after school.

The good deed and the height made her feel superior to the boys and girls playing stickball in the yard. All that effort just to hit and catch a silly little ball. All that hurrying just to step on a bookbag. One thing for sure, she told herself, even if the entire team fell upon their knees and knocked their heads at her feet in three reverent kow-tows, she would refuse to join them. Grandmother had the right attitude. The first and last time she went to see the cousins play the foreign game of basketball, the Matriarch had been horrified. "How uncivilized! How shameful! Children of Chungking's most honored clans fighting like thieves over a ball. Take me to the principal. With all that we pay, it is a disgrace that the school does not supply each student with a ball of his own to bounce."

"Shirley?" Mrs. Rappaport called, waving a paper. "Another perfect score. This time not in arithmetic, but in spelling. I am proud of you."

Shirley blushed. She could not get used to the American custom of receiving compliments with a simple thank you. It seemed so . . . impolite. But the Chinese way only confused people. Ever since Father had returned the compliment of the widow downstairs by insisting his wife was not in the least lovely, and in truth was only an old rag, the widow had stopped greeting him. Now she lay in wait to regale Mother with her own misfortunes at the hands of unappreciative men. Poor Mother! To avoid the woman she had to tiptoe down the hall like a mouse trying to escape the hungriest of cats.

Escape was the only route for Shirley, too. So she quickly put away the erasers and ran for the door.

Outside, she decided to cross the school yard like an emperor. It was time the others stepped aside for the Chinese. But then, not looking to the right or left, she did not see the runner stealing home base. They collided and fell. The catcher tagged the runner, shouting victory.

"Who the ***** do you think you are? You *********" Words Shirley had never heard before came spewing out. Words she was sure would never appear on Mrs. Rappaport's English list. This was big trouble. By the time Shirley and the angry one had gotten to their feet, all the other players had fled the scene.

Shirley stood her ground, but it took all her courage not to run, too. Mabel was a formidable sight. She was the tallest and the strongest and the scariest girl in all of the fifth grade.

"You *********. Why don't you ***********"

Shirley replied with a similar suggestion, in Chinese. Mabel did not hesitate a moment. She drew back her fist and punched Shirley square in the eye.

It hurt terribly, but not enough to make Shirley stupid. To trade punches with Mabel would be to box lightning. A most unequal match. So she borrowed a few more choice words from sayings coined by rickshaw pullers to insult riders who gave no tips.

Mabel was not intimidated.

"So you want more, you **********" A second blow, this time to the other eye.

Shirley considered fleeing. But emperors do not flee, and had a teacher not stepped through the school door exactly at that moment, one puny Chinese surely would have died right there and crossed over the Yellow Springs to greet her ancestors. But he did. As he started toward them, Mabel ran off in one direction, Shirley in another, as fast as she could go.

Safely home, but with two black eyes, Shirley knocked at the door.

When Mother opened it, she screamed. "What happened?"

"Nothing."

"Nothing?"

"Nothing important." She tried to slip into the bathroom.

"Oh no, you don't. Tell me exactly what happened."

Shirley bit her lips, but said not a word.

"Then, you just sit right there until your father comes home. He will find out what this nothing is all about."

Mother disappeared into the kitchen. She only returned when Father opened the door.

He did not scream. But he asked, very sternly, "What happened?"

"Nothing."

"Nothing?"

"Nothing important."

Mother tugged at his sleeve. "You must make her tell us everything."

"I shall."

But an hour later nothing was still nothing. To tell would be to tattle, and Shirley refused to tattle even on that giant of a no-friend of hers.

Finally Father stood up and announced that they were all going out.

"Where to, my husband?"

"To the police station."

Shirley could barely breathe. She had never spoken

to an American policeman before. Not even to ask directions. What would they do to her? Lock her up? Refuse her water? Maybe even pull her fingernails out?

Walking slowly behind her parents, she reconsidered her stand. What had she done so wrong? Nothing but walk and say a few words in Chinese. It was Mabel who should be going to the police station.

Mabel was!

Out of the corner of one battered eye, Shirley spotted the enemy stalking them. The look on her face was far from friendly, and Shirley did not need a lesson in reading faces to interpret its meaning.

> *"Squeal, your skin will peel.*
> *Tattle, your bones will rattle."*

Shirley caught up fast to her parents, then shuffled silently off to prison.

Just as they were about to enter, Father said, "This is your last chance to tell us what happened."

What should she do? On all sides, there was trouble. Mother stood to her right, Father to her left. Behind her, Mabel sat on a garbage can, watching her every move. In front of her, the monster of a building with iron bars.

Shirley opened her mouth then quickly thought better of speaking, and just shook her head. No matter how long the sentence, on the day of her release Mabel, as surely as tigers devour flesh, would still be around. Around to get revenge if Shirley Temple Wong dropped even the tiniest hint of what had happened that afternoon.

When the Wongs finally stepped inside the police station, Shirley gave thanks to the Goddess Kwan Yin. For there would be no nosy crowd to witness her trial. The station was empty except for a friendly policeman at the desk, who smiled and scratched his head throughout Father's explanation. After a few feeble attempts to interrogate her, he handed her a lollipop and sent the family home.

It was dark now and Mabel was nowhere to be seen.

Shirley refused to go to school for the next two days. Her mother thought it was because her eyes were almost swollen shut. Not so. Not so. Shirley needed the time for Mabel to realize that the Chinese had not squealed, and therefore her skin and bones deserved to stay intact.

The third morning, it rained. As Shirley opened her umbrella, she saw Mabel standing across the street underneath a tree, getting soaked. Oh no! The war was not over. Shirley started to run. But the tallest and the strongest and the scariest girl in all of the fifth grade was also the fastest, and easily caught up.

Shirley quaked.

"Hey, you okay?" Mabel's voice actually seemed rather friendly. The rainwater dripping down her black face looked like tears.

Could it be that Mabel was there to make peace? Shirley stepped back and replied uncertainly. "Okay. Okay."

"That's swell." Mabel clapped her hands and did something fancy with her feet. "Hey, okay if I walk with you to school?"

Shirley nodded, and hoisted the umbrella to cover Mabel's head.

When school was over, the skies had cleared and the walks were dry. Only the leaves, shined to a tender green, gave a clue to the shower that had passed over Brooklyn.

That afternoon Mrs. Rappaport had a teachers' meeting, so she dismissed Shirley with the rest of the class. Shirley had reached the top of the stairs when suddenly from nowhere Mabel appeared. "Hey, you wanna play stickball?"

Shirley turned to see whom the girl was asking. No one else was around. "Me?"

"Yeah, you. How about it?"

Shaking her head, Shirley smiled and started down the steps. Mabel, riding on the handrail, whizzed by and blocked her progress on the first landing. "Why not?"

"Dumb hands. No can catch." Shirley slipped past and continued on, only to find the way blocked again on the second landing.

"Nothing to it. I'll show ya."

Shirley shook her head again.

"Come on, it's fun."

"Yes, fun. But nobody take me on team."

"Leave that to me."

Shirley still hesitated. But Mabel was hardly the patient sort and pulled her by the sleeves into the school yard. When the others saw her coming, they groaned.

"What ya want to bring the midget for?"

"Oh no, ya don't. Not on my team."

"Are you kidding me?"

"Yeah. She'd bow first and then ask permission to cop a fly."

"Send her back to the laundry."

"The only way she can get in this game is to lie down and be the plate."

Shirley was ready to leave quietly, but Mabel hissed through her teeth, "Who says my friend Shirley here can't play?"

Advancing with mighty shoves, she pushed each objector aside.

"You, Spaghetti Snot?

"You, Kosher Creep?

"You, Damp Drawers?

"You, Brown Blubber?

"You, Dog Breath?

"You, Puerto Rican Coconut?"

Mabel was most persuasive, for everyone named now twitched a shoulder to signal okay. "That's what I thought. And as captain, I get first pick and Shirley's it."

When the sides were chosen, Mabel pointed to a spot by the iron fence. "Shirley, you play right field. If a ball comes your way, catch it and throw it to me. I'll take care of the rest."

"Where you be?"

"I'm the pitcher."

"Picture?"

"Ah, forget it. Look for me, I'll be around."

Resisting the temptation to bow, Shirley headed for her spot.

Mabel's picture was something to see. First, hiding the ball, she gave the stick the evil eye. Then, twisting her torso and jiggling a leg, she whirled her arm around in a most impressive fashion, probably a ritual to shoo away any unfriendly spirits, before speeding the ball furiously into the hands of squatting Joseph.

Once in a great while, the stick got a lucky hit, but the Goddess Kwan Yin was again merciful and sent the ball nowhere near the fence.

After the change of sides, Mabel stood Shirley in place and told her she would be first to hit. Shirley would have preferred to study the problem some more, but was afraid to protest and lose face for her captain. Standing tall, with her feet together, stick on her shoulder, she waited bravely. Dog Breath had a ritual of his own to perform, but then, suddenly, the ball was coming her way. Her eyes squeezed shut.

"Ball one!" shouted the umpire.

"Good eye!" shouted Mabel.

Shirley sighed and started to leave, but was told to stay put.

Again the ball came. Again her eyes shut.

"Ball two!"

"Good eye!" shouted the team. "Two more of those and you're on."

Shirley grinned. How easy it was!

Sure enough, every time she shut her eyes, the ball went astray.

"Take your base," said the umpire.

Mabel came running over. "Stand on that red book-bag until someone hits the ball, then run like mad to touch the blue one. Got it?"

"I got."

Mabel then picked up the stick and with one try sent the ball flying. In no time, Shirley, despite her pigeon toes, had dashed to the blue bookbag. But something was wrong. Mabel was chasing her. "Go. Get going. Run."

Shirley, puzzled over which bookbag to run to next, took a chance and sped off. But Mabel was still chasing her. "Go home! Go home!"

Oh no! She had done the wrong thing. Now even her new friend was angry. "Go home," her teammates shouted. "Go home."

She was starting off the field when she saw Joseph waving. "Here! Over here!" And off she went for the green one. Just before she reached it, she stumbled, knocking over the opponent who stood in her way.

He dropped the ball, and Shirley fell on top of the bag like a piece of ripe bean curd.

Her teammates shouted with happiness. Some helped her up. Others patted her back. Then they took up Mabel's chant.

> *"Hey, hey, you're just great*
> *Jackie Robinson crossed the plate.*
> *Hey, hey, you're a dream*
> *Jackie Robinson's on our team."*

Mabel's team won. The score was 10 to 2, and though the Chinese rookie never got on base again or caught even one ball, Shirley was confident that the next time . . . next time, she could. And yes, of course, naturally, stickball was now her favorite game.

On Saturday, Mabel taught her how to throw—overhand. How to catch—with her fingers. How to stand—feet two shoes apart. How to bat—on the level.

On Sunday, Mabel showed her how to propel herself on one skate at a time, then pulled her about on both until Shirley had learned how to go up and down the street without a fall.

Until that day, Shirley had never really understood

something Grandfather had told her many times. "Things are not what they seem," he had said. "Good can be bad. Bad can be good. Sadness can be happiness. Joy, sorrow.

"Remember always the tale of Wispy Whiskers, who did not cry when his beautiful stallion ran away. All his neighbors, though, were certain that it was a sign from heaven of his ill fortune.

"Later, when the stallion returned leading a herd of wild horses, he did not boast of his newfound wealth. This time his neighbors were equally certain that it was a sign from heaven of his good fortune.

"Later still when his son broke his leg taming one of the mares, the wise man did not despair. Not even when behind his back all his neighbors spread the terrible rumor that anyone with even one droplet of Wispy Whiskers' blood was forever cursed by the gods.

"And in the end, only his son lived. For the sons of all the inconstant neighbors, being sound of body, were forced into military service and one by one perished in a futile battle for a greedy emperor."

How wise Grandfather was, Shirley thought. Only he could have foreseen how two black eyes would earn her the lasting friendship of the tallest, and the strongest, and the fastest girl in all of the fifth grade.

六

月

JUNE

I Pledge a Lesson to the Frog

It was almost summer. An eager sun outshone the neon sign atop the Squibb factory even before the first bell beckoned students to their homerooms. Now alongside the empty milk crates at Mr. P's, brown paper bags with collars neatly rolled boasted plump strawberries, crimson cherries and Chiquita bananas. The cloakroom stood empty. Gone, the sweaters, slickers and galoshes.

At the second bell, the fifth grade, as always, scrambled to their feet. As always, Tommy O'Brien giggled, and each girl checked her seat to see if she was his victim of the day. Susie Spencer, whose tardiness could set clocks, rushed in, her face long with excuses. Popping a last bubble, Maria Gonzales tucked her gum safely behind an ear while Joseph gave an extra stroke to his hair.

Finally Mrs. Rappaport cleared her throat, and the room was still. With hands over hearts, the class performed the ritual that ushered in another day at school.

Shirley's voice was lost in the chorus.

"I pledge a lesson to the frog of the United States of America, and to the wee puppet for witches' hands. One Asian, in the vestibule, with little tea and just rice for all."

"Class, be seated," said Mrs. Rappaport, looking around to see if anyone was absent.

No one was.

"Any questions on the homework?"

All hands remained on or below the desks, etched with initials, new with splinters, brown with age.

"In that case, any questions on any subject at all?"

Irvie's hand shot up. It was quickly pulled down

by Maria, who hated even the sound of the word "spider." Spiders were all Irvie ever asked about, talked about, dreamed about. How many eyes do spiders have? Do spiders eat three meals a day? Where are spiders' ears located?

By now, everyone in the fifth grade knew that spiders come with no, six or eight eyes. That spiders do not have to dine regularly and that some can thrive as long as two years without a bite. That spiders are earless.

Since Irvie was as scared of girls as Maria was of spiders, he sat on his hands, but just in case he changed his mind, Maria's hand went up.

"Yes, Maria?"

"Eh . . . eh, I had a question, but I forgot."

"Was it something we discussed yesterday?"

"Yeah, yeah, that's it."

"Something about air currents or cloud formation, perhaps?"

"Yeah. How come I see lightning before I hear thunder?"

"Does anyone recall the answer?"

Tommy jumped in. "That's easy. 'Cause your eyes are in front, and your ears are off to the side." To prove his point, he wiggled his ears, which framed his disarming smile like the handles of a fancy soup bowl.

Laughter was his reward.

"The correct answer, Maria," said Mrs. Rappaport, trying not to smile too, "is that light waves travel faster than sound waves."

Shirley raised her hand.

"Yes?"

"Who's the girl Jackie Robinson?"

Laughter returned. This time Shirley did not understand the joke. Was the girl very, very bad? So bad that her name should not be uttered in the presence of a grown-up?

Putting a finger to her lips, Mrs. Rappaport quieted the class. "Shirley, you ask an excellent question. A most appropriate one. . . ."

The Chinese blushed, wishing her teacher would stop praising her, or at least not in front of the others. Already, they called her "teacher's dog" or "apple shiner."

"Jackie Robinson," Mrs. Rappaport continued, "is a man, the first Negro to play baseball in the major leagues."

"What is a Negro, Mrs. Rappaport?"

"A Negro is someone who is born with dark skin."

"Like Mabel?"

"Like Mabel and Joey and . . ."

"Maria?"

"No, Maria is not a Negro."

"But Maria is dark. Darker than Joey."

"I see what you mean. Let me try again. A Negro is someone whose ancestors originally came from Africa and who has dark skin."

"Then why I'm called Jackie Robinson?"

Mrs. Rappaport looked mystified. "Who calls you Jackie Robinson?"

"Everybody."

"Then I'll have to ask them. Mabel?"

" 'Cause she's pigeon-toed and stole home."

The teacher nodded. "Well, Shirley, it seems you are not only a good student, but a good baseball player."

There, she'd done it again! The kids would surely call her "a shiner of apples for teacher's dog" next. Shirley's unhappiness must have been obvious, because Mrs. Rappaport evidently felt the need to explain further.

"It is a compliment, Shirley. Jackie Robinson is a big hero, especially in Brooklyn, because he plays for the Dodgers."

"Who is dodgers?" Shirley asked.

That question, like a wayward torch in a roomful of firecrackers, sparked answers from everyone.

"De Bums!"

"The best in the history of baseball!"

"Kings of Ebbets Field!"

"They'll kill the Giants!"

"They'll murder the Yankees!"

"The swellest guys in the world!"

"America's favorites!"

"Winners!"

Mrs. Rappaport clapped her hands for order. The girls quieted down first, followed reluctantly by the boys. "That's better. Participation is welcome, but one at a time. Let's do talk about baseball!"

"Yay!" shouted the class.

"And let's combine it with civics too!"

The class did not welcome this proposal as eagerly, but Mrs. Rappaport went ahead anyway.

"Mabel, tell us why baseball is America's favorite pastime."

Pursing her lips in disgust at so ridiculous a question, Mabel answered. " 'Cause it's a great game. Everybody plays it, loves it and follows the games on the radio and nabs every chance to go and see it."

"True," said Mrs. Rappaport, nodding. "But what is it about baseball that is ideally suited to Americans?"

Mabel turned around, looking for an answer from someone else, but to no avail. There was nothing to do but throw the question back. "Whatta ya mean by 'suits'?"

"I mean, is there something special about baseball that fits the special kind of people we are and the special kind of country America is?" Mrs. Rappaport tilted her head to one side, inviting a response. When none came, she sighed a sigh so fraught with disappointment that it sounded as if her heart were breaking.

No one wished to be a party to such a sad event, so everybody found some urgent business to attend to like scratching, slumping, sniffing, scribbling, squinting, sucking teeth or removing dirt from underneath a fingernail. Joseph cracked his knuckles.

The ticking of the big clock became so loud that President Washington and President Lincoln, who occupied the wall space to either side of it, exchanged a look of shared displeasure.

But within the frail, birdlike body of Mrs. Rappaport was the spirit of a dragon capable of tackling the heavens and earth. With a quick toss of her red hair, she proceeded to answer her own question with such feeling that no one who heard could be so unkind as to ever forget. Least of all Shirley.

"Baseball is not just another sport. America is not just another country. . . ."

If Shirley did not understand every word, she took its meaning to heart. Unlike Grandfather's stories which quieted the warring spirits within her with the softness of moonlight or the lyric timbre of a lone flute, Mrs. Rappaport's speech thrilled her like sunlight and trumpets.

"In our national pastime, each player is a member of a team, but when he comes to bat, he stands alone. One man. Many opportunities. For no matter how far behind, how late in the game, he, by himself, can make a difference. He can change what has been. He can make it a new ball game.

"In the life of our nation, each man is a citizen of the United States, but he has the right to pursue his own happiness. For no matter what his race, religion or creed, be he pauper or president, he has the right to speak his mind, to live as he wishes within the law, to elect our officials and stand for office, to excel. To make a difference. To change what has been. To make a better America.

"And so can you! And so must you!"

Shirley felt as if the walls of the classroom had vanished. In their stead was a frontier of doors to which she held the keys.

"This year, Jackie Robinson is at bat. He stands for himself, for Americans of every hue, for an America that honors fair play.

"Jackie Robinson is the grandson of a slave, the son of a sharecropper, raised in poverty by a lone mother who took in ironing and washing. But a woman determined to achieve a better life for her son. And she did. For despite hostility and injustice, Jackie Robinson went to college, excelled in all sports, served his country in war. And now, Jackie Robinson is at bat in the big leagues. Jackie Robinson is making a difference. Jackie Robinson has changed what has been. And Jackie Robinson is making a better America.

"And so can you! And so must you!"

Suddenly Shirley understood why her father had brought her ten thousand miles to live among strangers. Here, she did not have to wait for gray hairs to be considered wise. Here, she could speak up, question even the conduct of the President. Here, Shirley Temple Wong was somebody. She felt as if she had the power of ten tigers, as if she had grown as tall as the Statue of Liberty.

七

月

JULY

Toscanini Takes a Walk

"Have a good time!"

"Take care!"

"See you in September!"

On the way home that last day of school, Shirley heard their voices echoing. Beset, she wavered. Sometimes she ran, couldn't wait to get away. Sometimes she dallied, turning back for one more glimpse of P. S. 8.

Without books to carry, her arms were free. But to Shirley, they seemed to sway from her shoulders as awkwardly as a chimpanzee's. Without stickball, the school yard had an eerie look, as desolate as Chungking during an air raid. Where had everyone gone? Mabel was not due at her grandmother's house in North Carolina until next week. Tommy's cousins did not expect him before Saturday. Only Maria had to catch a bus. There had been enough players. But each had replied, "Oh I can't, not today."

All had changed. Vacation was here. Her classmates had plans, plans that included their clansmen, not her. For the first time in a long while, Shirley thought of the courtyards. If only they were not so far away. She could join her own cousins and go skimming in a dragon boat, attend parties in honor of the Weaving Maid, visit temples set above the clouds, enter contests for hoisting the highest kite, harvesting the most silk cocoons. Surely they would welcome her . . . surely.

Suddenly she felt a tiny stab of fear. Had they forgotten her too? She vowed to answer Fourth Cousin's letter that afternoon. It had lain on the table for months. There was always so much to do, so little time. Also, writing in Chinese had become a chore. Too many of the characters were lost to her now. Again, that fear. Mother was right. She must never forget China or lose her Chinese.

But then, Shirley stuffed her hands in her pocket—and fingered the report card. Slowly, pride took hold. She had passed every course, and had gotten A's for effort. Mother would be delighted. Father would present her with a surprise. And tomorrow, she could sleep late, read books she had picked herself, even do nothing if she pleased. And almost every day, there would be baseball games on the radio, games to listen to all summer long.

So what if she did not see her friends until September. She had Mother and Father and Señora, not to mention Toscanini. Shirley had plans too. Lots of them. Like playing the piano and reading. She might even learn to knit. Yuck! Well, perhaps not that.

Determined to have a good summer, she raced the rest of the way home.

Before long, Shirley was infected by a most severe case of Dodger fever. Not even strawberry ice cream could lure her away from the radio when Red Barber was broadcasting the latest adventure of de Bums. Truly nothing else mattered. Not the heat that glued her skin to the plastic chair, not an outing to the beach, not even a movie followed by a beef pot pie at the Automat. Every time Number 42 came to bat, she imagined herself in Jackie Robinson's shoes. Every time the pigeon-toed runner got on base, she was ready to help him steal home. And when Jackie's sixteen-game hitting streak ended, Shirley blamed herself. On that day, she had had to accompany her parents to greet Mr. Lee from Chungking. Obviously, it was her absence from the radio that had made all the difference.

Neither Mother nor Father shared her enthusiasm. In fact, they welcomed the mayhem that emanated from the talking box as if it were a plague of locusts at harvest time. But none of their usual parental tricks succeeded in undoing the spell. What could possibly compete with the goose bumps Shirley sprouted each time Gladys Gooding and her organ led the crowd at Ebbets Field in the singing of "The Star Spangled Banner"? Shirley even talked the Señora into letting her off early to catch the final innings.

She had grown quite fond of the toothless Señora, who no longer bothered with the formality of dentures at all during their lessons. "In. No smile, no talk. Out. No eat. Probleema! Big probleema!"

Her initial impression of Toscanini had been more difficult to overcome, however. What a nag he was! Squawk, squawk, squawk. Even so, one sultry afternoon when the curtains hung perfectly still, she volunteered to take Toscanini for a walk.

"Walk?" repeated the Señora, smacking her head in disbelief. "Walk? Dogs go for walks. Cats, may bee. But never birds."

"In China, birds go for walks every day."

"They do? Toscanini has made one walk in all his life—from shop to here."

No wonder the bird had such a terrible disposition, Shirley thought.

"You tink he like?"

"Oh yes!"

"O-key do-key. You make walk."

Before appearing in public with Toscanini, however, Shirley had first to spruce up his cage. Its present condition would have shamed an elephant. Upstairs, she quickly dismissed Grandfather's practice of setting the bird free during the cleaning and inviting it back inside with a mere whistle. Toscanini was hardly the type to be trusted. Besides, if Mother ever came through the door to find a strange parrot whooshing about the apartment, she would faint away. What to do? What to do?

No probleema. With a pair of chopsticks, she removed what could be easily removed. With Father's toothbrush, she tackled the rest.

And Shirley was right. Toscanini loved walking. He blew out his chest to soak in the sunshine. He was sociable when strangers stopped to wish him a good day. He danced when Mr. P treated him to a handful of seeds. Not once did he flap his wings. Not once did he squawk.

She could not wait to report on the success of their maiden voyage to the Señora, but once back inside the basement, Shirley saw immediately that her teacher was in no mood to enjoy the details. Rocking back and forth, back and forth, the figure in black stared blankly ahead. The folds of her cheeks were drawn in a mournful pucker. On her lap was a letter. She never noticed that her pupil was back.

Instinctively, Shirley knelt by the rocker and took the Señora's hands in hers. "What's wrong, Señora?"

A tear fell and blurred the writing on the letter.

"Please don't cry, Señora. Please." Shirley wondered if she should go get her mother.

"Leetle girl, you are nice. Very nice. Like my Nonnie. She pretty too."

"Who's Nonnie?"

"My own leetle girl. She leeves far away in my old country. So far away."

Shirley could not bear to see the sadness on the Señora's face and lowered her gaze until it rested on the old woman's hands. Hands like those of Grand-grand Auntie, which she used to hold. Hands so old and so very far away. Suddenly, Shirley thought she would cry too.

"I weesh to be with my Nonnie. I weesh every hour."

"Why can't you?"

"Who care for house? No rent, my people no eat. So I stay. Like a watchdog with family away. Ten years now, I am watching. Ten years, without my Nonnie."

It was a lifetime. More years than Shirley had been alive, more years, perhaps, than Grand-grand Uncle had left in this world.

"Once I visit old country. I pay man to do for house. But he was bad. He steal rent. Now can never go back again."

Shirley looked up. "But you can go. You can. My

mother and father will look after the house. They are worthy. They come from an illustrious clan from the ancient civilization of China. Don't cry anymore. You can go to your Nonnie."

The idea pleased the old woman, for her lips parted until her pink gums showed in a huge smile. Then she giggled like a maiden. "Si! Si!"

"I knew you would see."

The probleema was solved. It was amazingly simple. All that was left to be done was to convince Mother and Father. Was this not proof of yet another great opportunity in modern America? Surely they could not possibly think this was just Bandit's scheme to escape the tyranny of piano lessons for the joys of Jackie Robinson!

八
月

AUGUST

Monsters

Within the week, Señora Rodriguez was happily on her way to Nonnie. Shirley barely recognized the woman who stepped into the taxi stuffed with suitcases stuffed with gifts. She wore a white linen suit and spectator pumps topped by a straw hat as smart as a lampshade. When she waved good-bye, her smile spar-

kled. A paste of Chinese herbs concocted by Mother had magically coaxed sore gums to adopt the twenty-eight intruders fashioned by the dentist.

Once the taxi disappeared from view, Shirley turned to her parents. "Will it be difficult taking care of this house?"

Father shrugged. "Probably not so difficult as raising a daughter."

"I will help. I promise."

"In that case"—Mother sighed—"kindly refrain from acquiring any more houses for the time being, my little landlord."

"Are you angry with me?"

They laughed. "Not at all. So long as we are collecting rents, we will not have to pay any."

"We're rich! We're rich!"

"Not quite," said Father with that smile. "The first month's rent has already been spent. A surprise for you."

"A whole month's rent just for me?"

"You've earned it."

"What is it? Can I have it now?"

"Patience. It will arrive soon enough."

That night, squeezed into her drawer bed like a step-sister's foot in Cinderella's shoe, Shirley could hardly sleep thinking of what the surprise might be. Not a piano, please let it not be a piano! The Señora had gone, but Toscanini was left in her care. If it was a piano, she must send a secret letter to China and tattle to the elders about her infamous piano lessons. Surely even a granddaughter who was a singsong girl would not do.

Perhaps it was a lifetime ticket to Ebbets Field? No, her parents would never take her there.

Another engine of some sort? That must be it, she thought. But what kind would be especially made for her? A bicycle? No, not expensive enough. An engine that would match her socks and hang up her clothes? She had never heard of one. A machine that would make strawberry ice cream? Now that would . . . She was asleep.

The surprise was delivered the next afternoon. It looked suspiciously like a sofa. A plain, ordinary sofa just to sit upon. Father must have seen the disappoint-ment on her face, because he quickly cautioned her. "It is not what it seems."

"It isn't?"

After the old sofa was removed and the new one was in place, he told Shirley to stand back and close her eyes.

She did.

When she opened them again, there stood a giant

bed fit for an emperor. Shirley threw herself on the mattress and lolled about like a fish tossed back to the sea. "How did you do it, Father? How?"

But before he could say a word, she shouted, "I know. It's just another wonderful engine made in America."

The first Saturday after the departure of the Señora, Shirley sat at the breakfast table hunched over the sports page of the *Herald Tribune*. Her hero had led the Dodgers to extend their winning streak to thirteen games. But what did the writer mean when he warned about the dog days of August?

"Shirley, let's go."

She looked up to see her father dressed in an old pair of pants and an even older shirt. Since he never went anywhere except in a handsome suit and jaunty bow tie, Shirley was surprised.

"Where, Father?"

"To work."

She was more puzzled than ever. Only other engineers understood what her father drew on blue paper. And he never dressed like this for the office.

"Hurry! It's about time we landlords took a good look at the property. We'll start with the furnace room."

Standing in the dimly lit basement while her father tried one key after another, Shirley was glad she was not alone. The strangest noises oozed from behind the locked door. Perhaps Nonnie was not the real reason the Señora had been so anxious to leave. Perhaps there was a monster. One who dined on little girls and had terrible indigestion.

The door creaked open. Father disappeared into the darkness. "I wonder where the light switch is?"

Please let him find it quickly, she prayed. Shirley had to will herself to stay put. Surely that was the flash of the monster's claws! Oh please!

"There, that's better."

The dungeon held no monster, but it was a beastly mess. The walls were stone, dirty and damp. The ceiling was cluttered with pipes that dripped, dripped, dripped and enough spider webs to keep Irvie content for a year. Piled high everywhere was junk, metal skeletons of forgotten species. In one corner stood a black iron box the size of several coffins. In another, huge rusty canisters. Underfoot, pools of murky water slick with oil. Fearing lizards and rats, cockroaches and snakes, Shirley hastened to her father's side.

"Yuck! This is horrible."

But Father did not seem to hear. He grinned as if he had unearthed a store of treasures, banging a pipe here, examining a wire there. "This will be a wonderful challenge. Just wonderful."

Had Father gone loco?

Throughout the game with the Cubs, they worked. Sorting, cleaning, stacking, drying, saving, discarding, boxing. Throughout Shirley wished she had never heard of Nonnie. She longed for her old drawer bed. The emperor could keep his.

The worst part of it was that Father did not even notice her unhappiness, her goodness. He hummed as he puttered. How could grown-ups be so blind to the pain of those younger and shorter than they? It was not fair.

If only she had a fever, then she could rest. Mother would wait on her, making sweet-and-sour soup and all the things she liked to eat. Father would buy her presents. She could listen to the radio. But she almost never had fevers. So that was that.

"Shirley, come here and help me with this."

"Yes, Father."

It was many evenings and weekends before Shirley realized the treasure her father had mined from the basement. With his alchemy of ingenuity and patience, he transmuted the junk into valued presents for every tenant who lived at Number Four Willow Street. A toaster for Professor Hirshbaum, who knew everything about everything except how to cook. A sewing machine for nearsighted Mrs. O'Reilly, who was forever tailoring old clothes for her triplets, Sean, Seamus and Stephen. A vacuum cleaner for Mr. Habib, who prized his carpets from Persia almost as much as his poodle, Mademoiselle F. P. At one time the initials had stood for Fifi Pompadour, but of late the pet had been known to all who shared the halls as Mademoiselle Faultee Plumbing. A fan for Widow Garibaldi, who now made Father an exception to her rule that men were never, ever to be trusted. An exercise machine for Mr. Lee, the 98-pound weakling.

Meanwhile, in her role of unhappy helper but obedient daughter, Shirley had become quite adept with tools and familiar with the inner workings of the old house. What she could possibly do with her knowledge of the intake valve, the Phillips screwdriver, the temperature cutoff, the ground wire, she did not know. But Father's pride in having raised a handygirl sometimes seemed worth the trouble.

There was one task, however, from which Father excluded her. He was much too meticulous an artist to permit so unsteady a hand to apply even a drop of paint to his hallways.

And so the Goddess Kwan Yin at last showed her mercy. While Father painted the halls a lovely pale beige, Shirley was free to add her howls to the protests against Enos Slaughter of the Cardinals, who had deliberately gone for Jackie Robinson's leg instead of first base and spiked her hero. It was a heartbreaking game, and the Dodgers lost. But Robinson would not be sidelined, and de Bums took the next five. The pennant was within sight.

One evening while Father was out and Shirley was pasting clippings in her Dodgers scrapbook, the lights suddenly went off. Yes, of course, naturally, Mother screamed.

Every tenant was shouting up the stairwell. Mademoiselle yapped. Toscanini squawked. Sean, Seamus and Stephen cried.

Shirley took charge. "Don't worry, Mother. I know just what to do."

"You do? What is it? Do it quickly!"

At every turn, Shirley collided with her mother. "Sit down, Mother. I will first go into the kitchen to turn on the stove. Then I will light a candle and change the fuses in the fuse box."

"Fuses? What's fuses?"

"Never mind." Shirley's tone befitted her superior knowledge. "You'll see. Within minutes the lights will all go back on."

"Hurry! Hurry!"

With key ring in one hand and candle in the other, Shirley made her way past the frantic tenants to the basement.

There, she inserted the key into the lock. But as the door swung open, out went the flame. Onto the floor dropped the candle. Vanished, her confidence. It was darker than an underground cave on a moonless night. The familiar noises of the boiler and pipes no longer sounded so innocent, and though she knew spiders and vermin no longer lurked within, she pictured them, multiplied and magnified, waiting to take revenge upon the little landlord who had so callously ousted them from their ancestral homes.

Her legs felt like spaghetti out of a can. The keys jingled in her hand. When she swallowed, it was her heart.

Amitabha! Why had she been so quick to show off again? Next time, she would hold her tongue. Next time . . . if there ever was a next time.

But done was done. She had to finish what she had started. Just a few steps to the fuse box. She must. She would. She had to.

Pocketing the keys, she felt her way along the walls. Was it her imagination, or did they feel wet and sticky, like blood?

Hand over hand she moved along the walls, stopping at each step to explore the surface, searching for the door to the fuse box. She should have reached it long ago. Who had moved it? If only she had a gourd to ward off the wicked spirits that delight in displacing everyday things. If only she had worn a talisman to insure her long life. But she was defenseless against all the demons of the dark. Defenseless even against her own thoughts, which told her that the walls were clammy with goo. Goo, like the innards of little girls.

It seemed as if weeks had passed, as if she had inched along the entire length of the Great Wall of China, which the emperor had built to keep out the barbarians, all fifteen hundred miles of it, when she heard her father's voice. "Shirley? Shirley?"

Like a criminal pardoned at the gallows, she ran from the scene, hand over hand, along the walls, up the stairwell. "Father! Father!"

Between the second and third floor landing, she fell into his arms. "I thought you might need some help," he said, as matter-of-factly as if saying "Good morning."

Shirley took a deep breath, then waited for her voice to return. "I certainly could have done the job alone.

Changing fuses is easy, but maybe with the two of us, it will go quicker."

"Yes, indeed."

With the aid of his cigarette lighter, the mission was accomplished without mishap.

But when the lights returned, Father screamed.

Fearfully, Shirley looked around. Were there monsters after all? But no. To her horror she saw that the sticky goo had been no figment of her imagination. Unbeknownst to her, Father had painted the furnace room and the paint had not yet dried. Now everywhere Shirley looked were little red palm prints—little red palm prints, like a school of exotic fish, swimming down the halls and up the stairwell.

Upon further study, she thought her handiwork rather dazzling. Most original. A masterpiece, even. If only . . . if only the other tenants of Number Four Willow Street could be made to think so too.

But, alas, like that of so many great artists in history, Shirley's genius went unrecognized. Her masterpiece soon lay unseen beneath several new coats of ordinary house paint.

九
月

SEPTEMBER

Secrets

The Dodgers were 7½ games ahead of the second-place Cardinals when the dog days of August ended. Alas, Toscanini had not fared as well. He looked awful, really chewed out, a shadow of his showy self. Much too much of him now feathered the bottom of his cage.

Shirley worried.

Father cited scientific proof that birds often molt during hot weather.

Mother filled Toscanini's cup with another herbal brew. This one, she assured Shirley, had successfully cured thousands of Chinese of baldness. "Wait and see!"

"Yes, Mother."

But as soon as her mother's back was turned, Shirley secretly dumped the concoction. Not because of a lack of faith in her mother's remedies. Just the opposite. She was sure the Señora would rather find upon her return a parrot, however bald, than Toscanini with yards of straight black hair.

Shirley was still worrying the night before the first day of school. Everything had been readied—new shoes that did not pinch, spiral notepads that rustled like dollars from the bank, and yellow pencils sharpened to a decimal point, without a tooth mark to be found. Yet . . . and yet, she was uneasy. The problem was not just Toscanini. What was it then?

As she lay in the dark, her thoughts flitted here and there, never staying for long, like the glow of fireflies on a late summer's eve. Vacation had sped by as swiftly as an arrow. But she liked school and certainly missed all the friends she had made there. Why was she shy about seeing them again?

Shirley hid her face in the pillow. She knew the answer. She was afraid her friends might have changed, just as change had come to her. It was true, she no longer thought so often about Fourth Cousin, once her best friend. And lately, almost not at all about the other cousins.

She still spoke Chinese with her parents, but even then foreign words were substituted for those that did not come easily. Mother corrected her. "Make an effort, Shirley. You must not forget you are still Chinese."

"Yes, Mother." But then out would pop another English expression, one for which there was no Chinese equivalent—Gee whiz! Baloney! Just for kicks! Party pooper! Fat chance! What's up?

For a moment, Shirley had the urge to look in the mirror. She hardly ever did that, not like some others she had seen in the girls' room fussing with themselves as if a stray hair could send them to jail. Did she look different now? Now that she was thinking more and more in English? Was her black hair turning blond? Was her nose getting higher? If she had a choice, she'd just as soon stay the same. Not that there was anything wrong with looking different, but she was used to the way she was. Lately the tenants had begun remarking on how grown up she looked. She wasn't sure she approved.

What was wrong with Shirley Temple Wong, as is? Nothing.

Yet . . . and yet, she was worrying about things that had not happened, just like grown-ups. It was awful.

Yawning, she closed her eyes.

When she opened them, she was in Chungking, walking up the Mountain of Ten Thousand Steps. The fog was dense, like steam from the bowels of the earth. She did not know if it was dawn or twilight, an in-between time. Her legs felt heavy, as if she were wading through deep water. She came to a fork in the road, one she remembered well, but now she could not tell which path was the way home. She looked to the east and thought she heard her mother call, "This way. This way." She looked to the west and thought she heard her father call, "This way. This way." Confused, she did not know how to choose. Then she thought that perhaps she had imagined it all, for suddenly the voices were gone and she was afraid to venture down either path and be lost.

Better go back, she thought. She had come too far. No telling whether the voices were fox spirits, imitating the voices of loved ones, out to entrap her.

She turned and ran. Ran until she bumped into a wall. It encircled her. She could see over it, but it was too high for her to scale. On the other side she recognized Fourth Cousin, and all the other cousins. They stared at her, a look of disgust on their faces.

"It's me, Shirley Temple Wong. It's me, Sixth Cousin. It's me, Bandit. Let me out. Let me in."

Her clansmen pointed and began to laugh. She called their names, reminded them of the memories they shared. There was no sign that they understood a word. When she waved her hands frantically, they did too. When she jumped up and down, they did too. When she cried out, they did too. They were all making fun of her.

Eventually she noticed Grand-grand Uncle. He was painting. She leaned over the wall and pleaded with him to set her free. He nodded to himself, happy with his work. The children studied the painting, then her. They howled with pleasure.

At last, he was finished and held up the picture. It was of a strange creature—a pigeon-toed bird with scanty green feathers and red palms. It was Shirley.

"Shirley, Shirley, wake up. It's time to go to school. Wake up."

She threw her arms around her mother and could not stop trembling.

"What's the matter? Did you have a nightmare?"

Unable to speak, she nodded.

"It was nothing. Just a dream." Her mother's voice was soft, so welcome to her ears.

When, finally, composure returned, she asked, "You would know me anywhere, wouldn't you, Mother? No matter how I had changed. You would, wouldn't you?"

"My daughter, I'd know each hair on your head."

By the time Shirley had entered the sixth-grade room of P. S. 8, she had forgotten the nightmare and, with it, her fears. At Mr. P's Tommy O'Brien had snuck up from behind to tug a braid. "Hey, Chop Suey, how are you doey?" Grinning, he then bowed deeply. She thought it rather wonderful that he remembered something she had done so long ago. Mabel joined them. "What do you know, de Bums are sure doing the job!" She jumped up to snatch an imaginary ball and sent it flying before her feet touched the ground. Joseph came huffing. "Hey, wait up!" He had gotten even rounder. Maria offered them a fistful of Double Bubble gum. Even Irvie sort of waved from across the street.

It was a new classroom, but they all took their old seats and talked about who their new teacher might be. When Mrs. Rappaport walked in, the class cheered.

"No use breaking up a winning team!"

While books were being passed out, the principal came in with a new student. "Class, this is Emily. Emily Levy."

Shirley knew immediately that they would be friends. Emily had huge blue eyes that were magnified even larger by a pair of horn-rimmed glasses, and she was the only other girl in class, besides herself, who wore two long braids. Though plain, she did not look at all like Fourth Cousin. Yet . . . there was something about her that reminded Shirley of her once-favorite companion. Perhaps it was the impression they both gave of no nonsense.

Their friendship began at lunch, when Shirley showed Emily where to buy tickets and took her through the line, whispering who among the counter ladies gave generous portions and what was good to eat and what should be avoided at all costs. "The corn muffins are the same ones from last year. Never, never touch the rice pudding."

Seated, Emily gave an efficient shake of her milk carton and asked without further ado, "Do you like to study?"

Shirley looked around to see if anyone had heard or could hear, but before she could answer, Emily confessed, "I do. I don't play anything but board games or charades. I read books, lots of them. I practice the cello two hours a day. My father's a psychiatrist. My mother's a committeewoman. I have two older brothers and sisters, and we all are progressives." Throughout her recitation, her blue eyes never blinked. They just peered straight into Shirley's, as if testing her.

Shirley wanted to laugh, but thought better of it. Clearing her throat, she replied in tones worthy of a monk collecting alms. "I like to study. I play all games. I read books. I hate the piano. My father's an engineer. My mother's a landlady. I have eight cousins, and we all are Chinese."

The response was obviously satisfactory, for Emily took a bite out of her tuna fish sandwich.

It was only after Shirley went to Emily's house that

she understood what her new friend had said. A cello was a big violin that sat on the floor. A progressive was someone who called her mother and father by their first names. A psychiatrist was a doctor who never wore a white coat and kept an office in the basement of a brownstone house furnished with a desk, a chair and a leather couch and lots of books, but no glass-enclosed shelves of scissors, needles, vials, bandages or medicines, herbal or otherwise. A committeewoman wore charcoal sweaters and skirts of scratchy material and wrote notes on a bulletin board while talking to other committeewomen on the telephone. Board games were not played with a ball. Charades was fun.

Shirley's mother heartily approved of this new friendship, for never once did Shirley return from Emily's dirty, tattered or wounded. Never once without a borrowed book to read. Emily had the entire collection of Nancy Drew mysteries. Her brothers had every adventure that Zane Grey ever wrote. Best of all, the Levy family played chamber music every afternoon, thus broadening Shirley's cultural horizons. In the beginning, Shirley only listened politely, hunting for the tune, because all too often each instrument sang its own song and confused her. How do you

listen to several conversations at once? Still, she admired the ritual, envying the Levys the pleasure they
took in one another's company, wishing her cousins
lived nearby so she could have an orchestra of her
own.

Only one aspect of her friendship with Emily would
have displeased her mother, but she was not likely
to find it out, and so Shirley did not trouble herself
too much over it.

One afternoon, when they were alone in the house,
Emily closed her arithmetic book and whispered, "Can
you keep a secret?"

"Of course."

"Will you swear it in blood?"

Shirley thought it over and asked, "How much
blood?"

"Not much."

How much was not much, she wondered? Before
she had a chance to inquire further, Emily rushed out
of the room. She returned brandishing a long pin with
a pearl on one end.

"Give me a finger."

Shirley reluctantly offered a pinky.

With a quick motion Emily stabbed it, and while

Shirley stared at the blood oozing out, her friend performed the same operation on her own finger. Then solemnly pressing pinky upon pinky, she said, "Swear unto death that it will be our secret no matter what."

"I swear."

Unblinkingly from behind the glasses, Emily insisted, "Swear the entire oath."

"I swear unto dea . . ." Shirley hesitated. Grandmother had always forbidden the saying of that word. "Say it and the gods will be tempted to make it so." But how could she refuse now? Her best friend was waiting. Perhaps, she prayed, the gods only spoke Chinese, never studied English, would not recognize temptation in another language. ". . . death, that this will be our secret no matter what."

The corners of Emily's mouth lifted into a wicked smile. "Come!"

They tiptoed down the stairs past the living room, down the stairs to Dr. Levy's office. Emily put her ear to the door. Shirley did the same. She could not hear a sound. Emily carefully tried the knob. It turned and they slipped inside.

"Look out the window and see if anyone's coming."

Shirley did as she was told. A pair of trousers walked
by, followed by a dog, which stopped to sniff a tree.
The animal glared at her as if to ask, what are you
up to? Shirley ducked.

"Anyone there?"

"No."

"Then come quick."

Shirley turned but saw no one.

"Here, behind the desk."

She almost fell over the book that lay open on the
rug.

"Look. Isn't this a wonderful secret?" Giggling, Emily pointed to the page.

Shirley dared not look. What terrible thing warranted such precautions?

"Look!"

She did. "What is it?"

"Naked people!" whispered Emily.

Oh. Shirley looked and looked, but did not recognize anyone she knew. The pictures were more like road maps colored in blue and red than flesh and bones.

"You can see everything."

That was true. Livers. Lungs. Stomachs. Brains. Even an unborn baby. Yuck!

Not to spoil Emily's fun, Shirley pretended enthusiasm. "I've never ever seen pictures like these before."

"Of course not. This is my father's book. *Gray's Anatomy.* We can find out everything, just everything, reading it."

The book was thick, thicker than any dictionary. Shirley had no desire to read the small print and whispered, "I hear footsteps."

Now she could but watch as her friend performed the mad antics of a comedian in an old-fashioned movie—scurrying here and there, bumping into the furniture, tripping over her own feet, hiding the evidence and stealing up the stairs.

Panting in the safety of her room, Emily cautioned, "Remember, it's our secret."

No secret was ever so safe.

A secret, like a chore, always seems to lead to another, one even more troublesome than the first. Shirley's second secret began the night of the final encounter between the Dodgers and the Cardinals. Her team led the league by 4½ games, but their opponents were the defending champions and still had a chance to take the pennant. It wasn't going to be easy, not with Harry Brecheen pitching for the Cardinals. He had been the hero of the last World Series. Even before the players took the field, Red Barber's voice was hoarse with excitement.

Suddenly her mother claimed Shirley's attention. "Have you done all your homework?"

"Yes."

"Then, you won't mind doing something for Mrs. O'Reilly, will you?"

"Now?"

"Now."

"Do I have to?"

"I think it is an opportunity . . ."

Rats! Another opportunity.

"Mrs. O'Reilly has asked you to baby-sit tonight. The poor woman has not been able to go to church to do her good works since the babies came. Now that you are grown up and they live only downstairs, Mrs. O'Reilly thought you might like to earn some money."

Money? That was different.

"Does Mrs. O'Reilly have a radio?"

Mother nodded, smiling.

Well, then. It was a golden opportunity.

The moment Shirley walked into the apartment, Mrs. O'Reilly picked up her pocketbook and was ready to go. "Dinner's on the table. Their diapers are in their room. I should be back in about two hours. Any questions?"

Shirley could not think of any. The radio was in plain sight, on the table next to the armchair.

"Be good, boys, won't you? Shirley's here to take care of you."

Sean, Seamus and Stephen stopped pushing their toy cars around the floor to look up with identical sweet smiles and wave.

"Bye-bye, Mommy."

"Bye-bye, Mommy."

"Bye-bye, Mommy."

As soon as the door closed, Shirley turned on the radio and twisted the dial until she found the familiar sounds of the ball park. Nothing had happened in the first inning.

Better get acquainted, she told herself and kneeled on the floor to say hello. But she got no response to Hi, Sean, Hi, Seamus or Hi, Stephen. The three merely crawled around, crying "Beep-beep, beep-beep, beep-beep." When they sat perfectly still, each triplet was indistinguishable from his brothers. Now, in orbit, they were an endless multitude. The effect was far from relaxing.

Grabbing the nearest, Shirley tried to station him in a high chair. The baby weighed less than Precious Coins, but was a lot more grief. He drooled with delight at Shirley's foolish struggle to thread him into the chair. If the legs were in position, the head was turned the wrong way. If the head faced the right direction, the legs dangled over the table. If she begged the child to bend, he stiffened. If she begged him to straighten, he slouched, almost slipping through her hands. Compared to this, dressing an octopus would have been a cinch.

One seated, two more to go. In each case, the battle was prolonged and silent.

When all three were safely in their chairs, Shirley was exhausted, and Joe Garagiola hadn't beaten the throw but had spiked Jackie Robinson's foot instead and given all Dodger fans one more reason to hate the Cardinals. The stands were in an uproar. But nothing compared to the cries that now emanated from the triplets, each outdoing the other.

"My chair. I want my own chair."

"My chair. I want my own chair."

"My chair. I want my own chair."

Shirley didn't even know which one was Sean, Seamus or Stephen, much less their chairs.

"Okay. Okay." Shirley hurried to reverse the seating that had taken her an inning to accomplish.

"Beep-beep, beep-beep, beep-beep."

Stamping her foot, she shouted, "Which is your chair?"

All three pointed to the one facing the kitchen.

"That mine."

"That mine."

"That mine."

Third Uncle was right. Money did not rain from

the skies. But no baby was going to defeat her. She
picked up the nearest one and sat down at the table.
With one hand tight around his belly, she fed him
with the other. The process was messy, like pitching
coal onto a moving train.

Meanwhile Robinson came to bat and almost got
into a fight with the catcher, Garagiola. If it hadn't
been for the umpire, there would have been a riot in
St. Louis. Shirley longed for just such an official to

keep the peace among Sean, Seamus and Stephen. When one was not spitting out food, another was tugging at her skirt, while the third screamed for his car, which had rolled underneath the sofa.

By the fifth inning, she had finally restored the dining room to its original condition. Now with one man on base, her hero smacked the ball right out of the park. She yelled hooray. The boys did too. But when she had stopped, they kept on yelling.

"Hooray! Hooray! Hooray!"

"Please stop, please, please don't shout anymore."

She might as well have been speaking Chinese.

Somehow she managed to peel off their clothing, stuff them into pajamas, and put them to bed. Then, muttering thanks to the Goddess Kwan Yin, she flung her weary self into the armchair to seek solace in the uninterrupted enjoyment of the last inning.

No sooner had she done so than a chorus of cries issued from the bedroom.

"Sean's wet."

"Sean's wet."

"Sean's wet."

"Which one of you is Sean?"

Silence. Drooling.

Undoing the buttons from neck to toe, she looked

for signs of Sean, wishing that they were dressed like Chinese babies, with a handy slit in their pants. How much simpler life had been in Chungking, when all she had had to do was lift Precious Coins' legs over a chamber pot.

By the time Sean was found and sanitized, the game was over. The Dodgers had won, 4 to 3, but Shirley was much too beaten to enjoy the victory.

Within moments, Mrs. O'Reilly returned. Her sons were snoring peacefully. Not a limb moved. The warriors had fought the good fight and deserved a rest.

Shirley earned three dimes that shone in her palm as brightly as medals for valor. She couldn't wait to show them to her parents.

The next day, Father presented her with a piggy bank. "Now that you're earning money, you deserve a proper place to keep it."

While her proud parents watched, Shirley lovingly deposited the coins in the china pig.

Thereafter, twice a week, Mrs. O'Reilly did her good works, and twice a week, Shirley wrestled with Sean, Seamus and Stephen. For a while, the coins that jingled ever more loudly in the pig drowned out the taunts of the Terrible Threesome. But as the magic number— any combination of Dodger wins or Cardinal losses needed for the Dodgers to win the National League pennant—dwindled from 7 to 6 to 5 to 4 to 3, Shirley fretted. More and more, she longed to exchange the chaos of the downstairs apartment for the quiet of her own. The boys were no fans of the Dodgers, or of Shirley.

Drastic measures were called for. Before she went to baby-sit again, Shirley secretly substituted buttons for the coins in the piggy bank. Then, at Mr. P's, she armed herself with a fabulous array of candy. *Amitabha!* Bribery worked magic. Sucking sweets, the Terrible Threesome was no more. In their stead, the Tame Trio.

Bursting into her own apartment in triumph, Shirley found her mother still working on the accounts for the Señora and her father mixing paint. As usual, they stopped what they were doing to witness the grand ceremony of feeding the pig. Mother gave her a quick squeeze. Father patted her on the shoulder.

"Go on, Shirley. Go on."

"No. Wait," announced Father as he pulled a small blue book from his back pocket to give Shirley. On it were stamped many numbers and her name in gold.

"What is it?"

"Your own savings account at the Brooklyn National Bank. Open it."

On the first line was a deposit of $5.00, a week's grocery money.

"Now every time the pig is filled, you can go to the bank yourself and make a deposit. And every penny in the account will go to help pay for your college education."

"College?"

"Yes. It is not too early to plan. College is expensive, but it is the most valuable treasure a person can have. With a proper education, you can aspire to do anything you desire in America. Be a doctor or a teacher or . . ."

"An engineer?"

"Of course."

Passing her finger over the name in gold, Shirley pictured herself as a grown-up, saving a life on the operating table, teaching a class, building a bridge. The images thrilled her, for she saw them so clearly in her parents' eyes.

She wanted to tell them all that was in her heart, but how do you express such feelings? Americans, she knew, would simply say, "I love you." But Chinese never used the phrase. It was too obvious, too direct. Like a present on one's birthday rather than those her father gave for no reason at all. Americans would also kiss. They did it all the time, even in public. That also seemed wrong. Without her saying a word, her parents knew how she felt and this she understood. It was the essence of being Chinese. But Shirley wanted to find a special way, her own way. What could it be?

Mother came to the rescue by handing her the pig. She gave it the customary three shakes. This never failed to make her parents laugh. Suddenly, Shirley remembered the trick she had played, bribing the boys. This time when the dimes dropped, the sound was hollow. Counterfeit.

In the morning the shame had not gone away. It cast a stillness within her like the hush of new snow. She began to see things she had failed to see before. Once again, her parents had slept through the alarm. But only now did she realize it was because of the long hours they worked. Worked to keep a promise she had made for them to the Señora. Worked to build a new life for them in America. Worked without complaint, always with cheer. How could she have deceived them so?

Shirley confessed everything to Emily.

"You'll feel much better when the buttons are replaced."

"How?"

"I'll share my school meals with you until you have saved enough."

"You will?"

"That's what friends are for."

But things thoughtlessly done are never so easily undone. This Shirley learned the next time she baby-sat. Expecting candy and having none, the boys took turns unplugging the radio. Three against one was no contest. And so she missed the crucial game—the game that clinched the pennant for the Dodgers.

十
月

OCTOBER

The World Series

Brooklyn went berserk. The Dodgers were the champs
of the National League. Jackie Robinson was voted
"Rookie of the Year" by *The Sporting News.* Nothing
else mattered but the World Series.

Each day during the Series, at the sound of the school

bell, Shirley and her classmates dashed to Mr. P's to cheer their team. This was no game. This was war. Huddled on empty soda crates, they sweated out each play. A Yankee hit, a blow to the stomach. A run, a mortal wound. A Dodger steal, a seizure of enemy territory. A score, a hero's welcome.

When the Yankees won the first two games easily, Tommy made the mistake of saying, "De Bums played like amateurs." No one spoke to him after that except Shirley, who sensed his tough talk masked a loyalty as passionate as the others'. "You didn't mean it, did you?"

"Sure, I meant it. Amateurs. Girl amateurs, to boot."

The next game was the longest ever played in the history of the World Series—over three hours of hard hitting and fielding and running at Ebbets Field. If it had gone into extra innings, Shirley's heart would have stopped. The Dodgers finally edged the Bronx Bombers, 9 to 8. Relief swooped through the crowd like the news of a snowstorm on the morning when a report not yet written was due.

After the fourth game, "Cookie" was on the lips of everyone. It had nothing to do with chocolate chips. It had everything to do with a player named Lavagetto. He was called off the bench to pinch-hit with two outs in the ninth, two Dodgers on base after walks, and the enemy leading by one run. The Yankee pitcher was one out away from becoming a phenomenon so rare that it had never been seen before—the first man to pitch a no-hitter in the World Series. Lavagetto swung and missed. Shirley prayed. He swung again. At the crack of the bat, everyone jumped to his feet and did not breathe until the ball hit the concrete wall to drive in the winning runs. The Series was tied.

In the last inning of the fifth game, Mabel shook Shirley like a bottle of catsup, shouting, "Do it again. Bust this one outta the park, Cookie!" Unbelievable as it seemed, once again it was the Yankees 2 to 1, with two outs and Lavagetto at bat. But history would not repeat itself. He fanned. And the kids who had rallied at Mr. P's disappeared as silently as dandelion heads in the breeze.

Tommy almost got himself killed before a pitch was thrown in the sixth game on Sunday. "It's over. De Bums are through. Back in Yankee territory, they got as much chance as a guppie swallowing a whale." Even Shirley thought he had gone too far. She helped to push him out the door.

The game was endless. Thirty-eight men played before it was over. Maria set a record too. She chewed

Mr. P clean out of gum. The Dodgers led throughout most of the game, but everyone knew the Yankees were luckier than mice in a cheese factory. They could not relax until Red Barber announced a Brooklyn victory. Not even when there was only one out to go, Yankees trailing 5 to 8. Especially not when Joe Di-Maggio was swinging the bat with two men on base. He had already smacked a home run earlier and could get lucky again.

DiMaggio connected, walloping one 415 feet to left center. At that instant Shirley hated him as much as she hated Awaiting Marriage—even more. Then a miracle. A miracle that banished every unkind thought and filled her with wonder. Gionfriddo, charging from left field to the edge of the bullpen, reached behind the fence and robbed DiMaggio of his sure home run and a tied game.

Screeching and leaping, the fans at Mr. P's gave a good imitation of monkeys stung by a swarm of bees. Even the boxes of Ivory Snow and Corn Flakes, jars of peanut butter and mustard, hopped. Forgetting thirty-nine generations of Confucian breeding, Shirley hugged anyone in reach.

Mr. P swept her up in his arms and twirled to a song he bellowed out in Greek. Everybody started to clap in time. Around and around, faster and faster, until finally in happy exhaustion, he plopped her on the counter to mop his face with his apron. Mabel and Joseph took the floor. Like a yo-yo, the captain flung Joseph out and snatched him back. Mabel sure could jitterbug. Finally to Irvie's horror, Maria pulled him off the freezer and as he stood stiff as an icicle, she tap-danced about, nudging him with a shoulder, patting him on the cheek, closer and closer till they were nose to nose, and he fled into the street.

Only then did Shirley notice Tommy, outside, darting from car to car, kissing the hoods like a proud new papa. Any other day, it might have seemed strange. Not today. The Series was tied and the Dodgers had been reborn.

What happened on Monday was too painful to recall. On Tuesday Shirley could forget everything, except that the Dodgers had lost and the Yankees were the World Champs. Oh, she got up in the morning and went to bed at night and did what she was supposed to, but her heart wasn't in it.

Wait until next year, everyone said. Only next year seemed as far away as a balloon lost in summer skies.

十一月

NOVEMBER

Moon Cakes Without Grandfather

Leaning out the kitchen window, Shirley and her parents watched the crescent moon drift through the clouds. Below, a lone maple shivered in the wind, shedding leaf after leaf that scooted down the lane without so much as a backward glance.

No one spoke. All knew they were thinking the same thoughts. How could they have let the eve of the Mid-Autumn Festival slip by without realizing it? Americans did not commemorate the fullest moon of the year, but the Wongs had done so for centuries. If Grandfather had not sent the moon cakes, would they have remembered at all? True, the clan was far away and there was no courtyard to gather in, but that was all the more reason for them to recall the glow of reunion under the stars.

Each had an excuse. Mother had not been feeling well. Father had been toiling day and night to repair the leaks that sprouted throughout the house like chicken pox. And Shirley had been moping for weeks over the loss of the World Series. But no excuse eased the sadness that welled in their hearts.

Now the moon itself disappeared, swallowed by a fitful cloud. Father closed the window, and together the family returned to their seats at the dining table. On each plate was a golden moon cake filled with lotus seeds and honey.

Shirley started to take a bite, then stopped. She did not deserve such a delicious treat. A tear escaped, then another.

Mother dried her cheeks, smiling a brave smile. "Let

us pretend we were there, and tonight is the Fifteenth Day of the Eighth Moon. This table, the altar in the Garden of Celestial Harmony. This covering, not oil-cloth, but red brocade, embroidered by the ladies of the House of Wong. This bowl, not empty, but one of five filled with grapes, apples, peaches, melons and pomegranates, offerings to the gods for the longevity of our clan. The salt, incense. The pepper, candles. . . ."

"And all around," Shirley said, transported by the dream, "flowers. In the air, the smell of jasmine. Overhead, the biggest and the brightest of moons. So near that we can see the Hare that stands under the cassia tree pounding the elixir of life in a jade mortar. The paper lanterns are dancing in the willows while a musician plays on the lute. . . ."

"There sit my father and mother," Father continued, "surrounded by clansmen. The harvest is in and we are all together, from near and far, to celebrate with the reading of poetry the bond of all bonds—family."

Once again, no one spoke. But this time the silence was gentle, like a pause in a piece of beautiful music when one melody has ended and another is yet to begin.

At last Shirley spoke. "I wish . . ."

"What do you wish, my daughter?"

"I wish I were the girl in Grandfather's story."

"Which one?"

"The one about the filial daughter and the loving bride."

"My father tells so many, it's hard to be sure. Shirley, you tell it again. This, too, will bring us home."

She nodded, then began, telling it as Grandfather would, slowly.

Long, long ago, there lived a most honorable man who owed much of his good fortune to the kindness of his friend. And so when their wives were both with expectant happiness, they vowed, even before the babies left the womb, that should one be a girl and the other a boy, they would be married. And indeed a daughter and a son were born.

Before the children could crawl, the friend was named by the emperor to an important post in the Capital. On the day he left, his last words were, "When my son is of age, he will come back to claim his bride."

To which the father replied, "No other honor could make us as happy or as proud."

The years passed, and the child grew into a maiden

admired by all for her beauty and goodness. One day while she was walking by the river, she happened upon a young fisherman. Although they had never met before, they immediately knew that the Fates had decreed for them a love as faithful as the north star. And so, when it was time for him to go upriver, she ran away with him.

They lived happily as man and wife, but always there was sadness too. Not a moment passed that they did not think of her poor parents and the dishonor of a promise broken.

After they had been away ten years, the daughter implored her husband to return to her hometown. "I cannot live any longer without begging my parents for forgiveness."

When the boat anchored along the banks where they first met, the daughter asked the fisherman to go ahead to explain. He agreed, asking her to come along an hour later.

At the house, he fell upon his knees before his in-laws and confessed the wrong he and their daughter had done. The couple looked mystified. "How can this be? How can this be? Our daughter has never left home. She has always been at our side. She has never married, for her betrothed died in battle."

Now it was the husband who cried, "How can this be? How can this be?"

Precisely at that moment, the garden echoed with temple bells. In the distance were two women, one to the left of the cypress tree and one to the right. Slowly they walked toward each another. Beneath the evergreen boughs, the two figures merged into one. She came into the house and kow-towed three times before the fisherman and the old man and his wife. She was no stranger, but the love of their hearts. She was wearing two gowns. One that belonged to the fisherman's wife. One that belonged to the filial daughter.

For many moments, there was no sound save the hum of the refrigerator in the next room. Then Shirley said in a small voice, "It is so sad, moon cakes without Grandfather. When will we all be together again?"

"Perhaps someday."

"Someday soon?"

The question hovered in the air, hauntingly.

十
二
月

DECEMBER

A Star-Spangled Christmas

Shirley spent the weekend after Thanksgiving writing
a ten-page letter to her cousins in Chinese describing
her debut onstage as a turkey. She drew colorful illustrations to help even Precious Coins picture each scene
in the school play.

The transformation of a *Homo sapiens* into a *Meleagris gallopavo* had not just happened with a wave of the wand. It took two knitting needles, Mother's ingenuity and the resources of all the tenants. Father sacrificed his favorite brown sweater, which was unraveled and remodeled into the roly-poly hide of Tom Turkey. Mr. Habib donated the leather headgear and goggles he had worn as a pilot in the war, to which was attached a red tie belonging to Mr. Lee to simulate the bird's fleshy nose. Mrs. O'Reilly yielded a boa reeking of mothballs for the feathers. Sean, Seamus and Stephen lent their pillows to plump up the bump, hump and rump of the beast. Widow Garibaldi insisted on buying rubber flippers for the feet. Professor Hirshbaum tutored Shirley on the various movements peculiar to the breed.

"I wish you all could have been there!" Shirley wrote.

A few weeks after the show, Mrs. Rappaport announced another project—a class election for someone to represent the sixth grade at the Christmas Assembly. "The election will be held next Monday."

At lunch that day, Shirley watched Tommy show off even more than usual, swaggering from table to table, getting laughs.

"Hey, Four Eyes, be a sport and vote for me."

Emily ignored him, drawing the last of her milk through her straw with a series of loud slurps.

Tommy refused to be snubbed and, cupping his ear to the carton, shouted, "What's that? No kidding! You're crazy about me. Inside that answer machine all those brainy cells are rooting for me to win."

With hands clasped over his heart, Tommy feigned a swoon; then, leaping like the Frog Prince, he went off to entertain his older fans behind the lunch counter.

"How juvenile!" Emily muttered, studiously wiping her glasses with a napkin.

To cover up her own soft spot for Tommy, Shirley agreed, too heartily.

Glasses in place again, Emily stared, as if reading Shirley's thoughts, all knowing.

And so, before Shirley knew it, she was urging her friend to run herself.

"That would be an exercise in futility," Emily replied, in her most progressive voice. "Only you and I would cast votes in my favor."

It was true. Emily was not popular. She got all A's, never once got into trouble and seldom hung around.

Once again, Emily was cleaning her glasses, and Shirley's heart went out to her friend. "That's not true.

Lots of people like you. Wait and see. You can win."

"Do you really think so?"

"Of course I do."

That afternoon Shirley embarked on a campaign among the girls to elect Emily. She reminded them of all the pranks Tommy had played on them, of all the sterling qualities of the smartest student in their class, of why a girl, not a boy, should represent them. Mabel was a big help. Everybody looked up to her, so when she made Emily her candidate too, Emily had a chance.

When the secret ballots were counted, Emily won by a single vote, there being exactly one more girl than boy in the sixth grade.

To Tommy's credit, he was the first to congratulate the winner. "Nice going, pal. You won fair and square."

Shirley was thrilled. Emily came to school the next day with her hair in curls.

A week later, in the midst of rehearsing carols for the pageant, the principal came to make an announcement. "Boys and girls, I have wonderful news. This year for our Christmas Assembly we invited a special guest, and today he has agreed to come. Soon we'll all have the privilege of hearing him. And Emily Levy, as your elected representative, will have the honor of presenting him with the key to P. S. 8. I'll not keep you in suspense any longer. Our guest is Mr. Jackie Robinson!"

The cries of joy must have reached all the way to heaven, for just at that moment the first snow fell, swirling merrily outside the windows like confetti.

When the shouting had ended and the lesson resumed, Shirley found herself thinking how silly Emily looked in curls, rather like that batch of old springs Father kept in the basement. And each time her friend tried to get her attention, Shirley pretended to be solving the denominator. Then Emily passed her a note, which she pocketed without reading.

"Any questions?" Mrs. Rappaport asked.

Emily raised her hand.

"Yes?"

"I don't have a question about fractions, but may I ask you something else?"

"Of course."

Shirley wondered if Emily was going to do some showing off of her own.

"I'm grateful that my classmates have elected me their representative. But I think they would have chosen someone else if they had known that Jackie Robinson was going to be at the Assembly. I don't know a

• 161 •

thing about baseball. And Shirley knows everything there is to know about Jackie Robinson. So, if it's all right with the class, I think she should be the one to make the presentation. Not me."

Everyone clapped, but Shirley had never felt so ashamed. She was unworthy of Emily's friendship. She did not deserve the goodwill of her class. Unable to speak, she hid her face in her hands.

The next thing she knew, Mabel was up and chanting.

> "Hey, hey, you're just great—
> Emily Levy sure does rate.
> Hey, hey, you're the rage—
> Shirley's gonna be onstage."

Now, two weeks of delicious anticipation later, Shirley sat between the principal and the guest of honor onstage before an assembly filled to overflowing. Every seat was taken by a student or guest. Teachers, like proud shepherds, stood against the walls smiling at their charges, who looked equally pleased to be herded there.

Pressed against the windowpanes were cardboard snowflakes the size of the moon. The sunlight filtering through them dappled the hall with shimmering lace.

Overhead, paper garlands dipped from the chandelier, forming a canopy of red and green. At the back of the room were easels hung with paintings done by students—a snowman dancing, a Santa stuck in the chimney, a sleepy child searching the midnight skies, wooden soldiers come to life, a family praying over their holiday feast, reindeer soaring above the sky-scrapers of New York, a babe asleep in the manger. In the air was the scent of pine.

As the kindergarten class led the singing of carols, Shirley captured the scene for her memories.

She looked at the giant spruce that dominated the stage. Twinkling with colored lights, shiny balls, white doves, jeweled icicles, and miles of silver tinsel, it was topped by a brilliant star and skirted with gifts wrapped in finery. Compared to this, the one at home was positively scrawny, but to Shirley, it was special just the same. For on each bough hung a picture of a clansman, a reminder of the courtyards so far away.

Shirley's heart smiled as she recalled the night she and Mother and Father had trimmed their first Christmas tree. When it was done, Mother had announced, "Shirley, it is time you knew. I am with expectant happiness."

"*Amitabha!* I'm going to have a brother at last."

"Or a sister."

"But in my dreams, it is always a boy."

"Dreams or no dreams, it may yet be a girl."

For a brief moment, Shirley had considered that possibility, then dismissed it with a smile. "Until the doctor tells me I'm wrong, it is a boy."

She had begun to make serious plans. Yes, of course, naturally she would love him, cuddle him, feed him, walk him, diaper him, burp him, dress him, and be a big sister to him in every way. But as soon as possible, she would also teach him. How to speak—not just English but Chinese. How to write—not just the alphabet but characters. How to chew gum and blow bubbles. How to smack a homer and walk a yo-yo and skate backward. And she would tell him stories, the ones written in books, the ones that Grandfather told.

Most importantly, she would tell him about the life he would probably never know, the life she had once lived in Chungking. The taste of watermelon cooled in the well . . . the sound the willow branches made when the clansmen swept their ancestors' graves . . . the fragrance of perfumed fans . . . the touch of the fortune-teller's finger, tracing destiny along the palm of one's hand . . . the view from the House of Wong as the sun set over the Mountain of Ten Thousand Steps . . . and especially the people who lived on that far side of the world, to whom they would always belong.

Then the lilting strains of "Silent Night" brought Shirley back to Brooklyn, and she searched the audience for her parents. When she spotted them in the third row among all the tenants of Number Four Willow Street, she winked. The tenants wiggled their fingers at her. She blushed. Her classmates found this most amusing, for they whispered among themselves, then orchestrated a frenzy of waves for all to see. Only Emily and Mabel refrained from embarrassing her.

Emily and Mabel, her best friends. The ones who should have been on the stage in her place. For Mabel knew more about baseball than she. And Levy, not Wong, represented the best mind and the warmest heart in all of the sixth grade.

Poised between laughter and tears, Shirley took a deep breath to catch the high note in the last refrain.

". . . peace.
Sleep in heavenly peace."

In the brief silence that followed the song, Shirley suddenly realized that her moment would soon come.

How she had longed for it! But now that it was here, she felt unprepared—as if she had never pictured it, had not rehearsed it over and over again. Biting her lips, she looked anxiously at her hero, Jackie Robinson.

The handsome baseball player gave her a grand slam of a smile and put out all her fears.

Years later, Shirley could still remember the speech he gave, could still repeat word for word what she said when she handed him the huge golden key.

First came the words she had memorized. "To the Rookie of the Year, to the Dodger who made a difference, to the man who changed what has been, Mr. Jackie Robinson, a great American, I present on behalf of P. S. 8 the key to our school."

Mr. Robinson bent down and took the key she held out. "Thank you, Shirley," he said. "Thank you, everyone. I shall treasure this day."

When the cheering and applause ended, he spoke again. "Remember what I said in my talk—excel. For someday you will all hold the keys to making America the greatest country in the world. Someday I hope to be sitting in an audience like this and listening to one of you giving a speech as the President of the United States. . . ."

The great Jackie Robinson turned to Shirley and pat-

ted her on the shoulder. "Perhaps," he said with a smile, "it will be you, Shirley."

Shirley shook her head and insisted loudly, "Oh no! Not me. Not me."

"Do not be so pessimistic. Someday, Americans will elect a woman President."

"Yes. But it cannot be me."

"Why?"

"Because I'm not eligible."

"You're not?"

"No, sir. Mrs. Rappaport taught us that the Constitution of the United States clearly states that the President must be born in America, and I was born in China. But, Mr. Robinson, my brother who is not born yet, he can be President someday. He can!"

Only then did Shirley remember that they were onstage and everyone was listening. Now all she heard was laughter. Oh Merciful Kwan Yin, she prayed, make me disappear!

But Jackie Robinson would not let her go. He took her hand and raised it in triumph, shouting, "Hooray for the sister of our future President, Shirley Temple Wong, the American!"

The clapping that swept the hall seized her by surprise and she stood very still, wondering for a moment if she was imagining it all. No, this was happening. This was real. Instinctively, she bowed. When she lifted her gaze again, something was in her eyes and her vision blurred. Yet, as clearly as the flag that was draped from the balcony, she saw before her faces that had not been there a second ago. Grandfather, Fourth Cousin, Precious Coins and all her clansmen. They, too, clapped, just as they had done the night the Patriarch had given her an American name, at the dawn of the new year.

What a star-spangled Christmas this is! she thought. This year of 1947. The Year of the Boar. The year when dreams came true. The year of double happiness.